P9-CNH-501

AMBUSH AT BEDROCK

Someone was out to get Pace Larrabee! Someone had crippled him in an ambush, killed one of his men, and rustled a herd of horses . . . someone had stampeded his cattle and threatened to poison his water holes.

Pace had carved a thriving ranch in the wild, untamed wilderness of Oregon. He'd been helped by Arliss, the woman who staked him to a strange and passionless partnership, but he had to be wary of Gilgen, the man with a dark past and a strange hold over Arliss. And he had other enemies. Was his foe among the nesters who poached on the land back in the hills? Even their fiery women had their reasons for hating him.

One from among the enemy legion was about to step forth, one with an obsession and a deadly aim—to kill Pace Larrabee!

Giff Cheshire was born in 1905 on a homestead in Cheshire, Oregon. The county was named for his grandfather who had crossed the plains in 1852 by wagon from Tennessee, and the homestead was the same one his grandfather had claimed upon his arrival. Cheshire's early life was colored by the atmosphere of the Old West which in the first decade of the century had not yet been modified by the automobile. He attended public schools in Junction City and, following high school, enlisted in the U.S. Marine Corps and saw duty in Central America. In 1929 he came to the Portland area in Oregon and from 1929 to 1943 worked for the U.S. Corps of Engineers. By 1944, after moving to Beaverton, Oregon, he found he could make a living writing Western and North-Western short fiction for the magazine market, and presently stories under the byline Giff Cheshire began appearing in *Lariat Story Magazine*, *Dime Western*, and *North-West Romances*. His short story *Strangers in the Evening* won the Zane Grey Award in 1949. Cheshire's Western fiction was characterized from the beginning by a wider historical panorama of the frontier than just cattle ranching and frequently the settings for his later novels are in his native Oregon. *Thunder on the Mountain* (1960) focuses on Chief Joseph and the Nez Perce War, while *Wenatchee Bend* (1966) and *A Mighty Big River* (1967) are among his best-known titles. However, his novels as Chad Merriman for Fawcett Gold Medal remain among his most popular works, notable for their complex characters, expert pacing, and authentic backgrounds. A first collection of Giff Cheshire's Western stories, *Renegade River*, was published in 1997 and edited by Bill Pronzini.

AMBUSH AT BEDROCK

Giff Cheshire

FIC CHE

Cheshire, Giff, 1905-

Ambush at Bedrock

GUNSMOKE

Hemet Public Library
300 E. Latham Ave.
Hemet, CA 92543

Jun 2006

First published in the UK by Arrow Books

This hardback edition 2006
by BBC Audiobooks Ltd
by arrangement with
Golden West Literary Agency

Copyright © 1969 by Giff Cheshire.
Copyright © 1970 by Giff Cheshire in
the British Commonwealth.
All rights reserved.

ISBN 1 4056 8075 X

All of the characters in the book are fictitious, and any
resemblance to actual persons, living or dead, is
entirely coincidental.

British Library Cataloguing in Publication Data available.

Printed and bound in Great Britain by
Antony Rowe Ltd., Chippenham, Wiltshire

AMBUSH
AT BEDROCK

CHAPTER 1

The horse, a white-stocking roan, poked its way toward headquarters pretty much to suit itself. Its rider sat the saddle like a tired Indian, head hanging forward, shoulders sagging, legs loose and dangling. The horse was in Cob Durnbo's string and, that afternoon, Cob had been sent to Pistol Peak to bring in some horses that had wintered there. Now both the horse and its rider were returning without the horses from the hills, and Cob rode like he was asleep or drunk.

Pace Larabee cursed, holding it under his breath out of respect for feminine ears in the room behind him. Cob could be drunk *and* asleep. He had been one of the men Pace had let visit town before the long, uninterrupted job of calf roundup began. Including Durnbo, they had all come back in varying states of repair the day and night before. They were good men and tough enough to ride a hot-spot range like the Bedrock, which also made them hard to discipline. Pace shut his eyes to the inevitable bottles stashed around the ranch after such an excursion. But every man of them knew that, if he wanted his time, getting a snoot full on the job was a sure way to draw it.

Pace swung from the window and headed for the door, moving heavily on his bad leg. His face showed more temper than he realized, for the girl in the room said quickly, "What got into *you,* all at once?"

"Nothing, Arliss," he said over his shoulder. "Back in a minute."

"You better be," Arliss said in her lazy voice. "I didn't ride all this way to sit by myself and rock, this evening."

From the big house front porch Pace got a better look at the horse and rider coming across the bottom meadow. Even in the twilight of an Oregon April, he could detect a spent, slack distress in the man swaying in the saddle. The truth of it hit him with an impact like that of the rifle slug that had come off the rimrock, the fall before, and crippled his knee. He stood there for a breath, gathering it in, then swung heavily down the steps into the yard. He saw Bim,

7

his younger brother and daytime *segundo,* over by the bunkhouse.

Bim stared at him curiously but, saying nothing to him, Pace swung on by him to the corrals. There was no use rushing onto the meadow to meet the white-stocking horse. One of those kept up through the winter, it was heading toward him, full of hunger and indifferent to whatever new problem it was bringing in.

Cob had straightened up in the saddle and, for the moment, nothing looked wrong with him. Bim came up beside Pace and read the situation for himself. He stood scowling and silent. He wasn't a small man but seemed so beside Pace and looked young and boyish for the job he held down on the ranch. Nearing the feed corral, the white-stocking broke into a trot. Cob lurched in the saddle and grabbed the horn.

Bim bolted forward, with Pace following on his stiff knee. Closer, he saw that Cob's cotton shirt was soaked with blood. His thin brown face was wrenched in strain and pain, and his eyes were glazed with the burden of his experience, whatever it had been. He looked at Pace and gasped, "Gone. Every goddam critter." There was a rattle in his voice. "Followed the sign. It run up Cobble Crick. Then—wham—off the rim—"

Pace said sharply, "Again?"

"Again."

Cob's head rocked forward. He was far worse hit than Pace had been, and it had taken all he had to get home.

They lifted him down and carried him to the bunkhouse. For the past few weeks the spring violets had been appearing, and extra cowhands had drifted in to sign on for another season's work on the range. So there were ten men in the poker game that the opening door broke up. None of them had sensed anything wrong outdoors.

They stood in benumbed silence while Pace and Bim carried in the bloody puncher and put him down gently on his bunk. Bim said in a chilled voice, "Ride for the doc, Charley. Spike, get some hot water and rags. Who's got some whiskey cached somewhere?"

Pace had put his finger on Cob's wrist. He shook his head. "No use. He's dead."

He straightened and looked at his brother through a long moment. Maybe this would change Bim's mind about some things that had kept them on the outs for months.

Charley Varley looked at Bim, too, and said heavily, "I reckon I better make that the sheriff."

Pace looked up with anger in his face. They all knew

8

how helpless the law was against the element in the upper Bedrock basin. Half-squatter, half-outlaw and, according to his own view, half-wolf. Yet this was a killing, and there were formalities. So he kept silent when Bim nodded Varley an affirmative answer. Then he turned and walked out.

Arliss was still in the lodgelike main room of the big house and still unaware of what had happened. Her last name was Markle, she lived in Rowel City, and was his silent, usually absent partner. She had lighted a lamp against the coming night, and its soft rays made her dark face even prettier. She turned toward him with an easy swing of her tall, slim body. Seeing the look on his face, she asked, "What's wrong?"

"Dead man in the bunkhouse," Pace said wearily. "Another shot from the rimrock."

He explained what little he knew from what Cob had managed to say. The rest came from his own familiarity with ranch operations and the makeup of the back country and its denizens. There had been eighteen head of horses in the band the puncher had gone to bring in for the roundup. They would be worth twenty-five hundred even on a shady market somewhere.

Arliss said musingly, "That sort of knocks out the idea you were shot by a tramp horse thief."

"You know I never believed that. Bim does, if this hasn't changed his mind, because he's got an eye on a girl or two up there. The sheriff does because it's the easiest way to close the case. This proves it's more than that. Maybe more than we've seen even now."

Pace forgot her in the dark thoughts his remark had started. The ranch had lost a horse or two now and then before. It had lost even more cattle which, as beef, had gone into back-country bellies. There had been other kinds of mischief, too, because a big outfit was always hated by the ne'er-do-wells around it.

That could be written off as a nuisance, had things not taken a deadlier turn. Pace had been on Bear Prairie, that cold October day, just keeping his eye on things. The shot that had changed everything for him personally had come without warning. It had been aimed to put him where Cob was now, he was certain, but it had only turned him into a gimpy.

Arliss broke in on his thoughts, saying, "What do you mean—more than we've seen even now?"

"You won't like this. I think your friend Gilgen's behind it. He spends a lot of time in the back country."

Her face darkened. "There are girls up there. Bim's not the only one who's found that out." She glanced at him thoughtfully. "Why call him *my* friend?"

"I see him around your place a lot, too."

"It's a place of business. Why should I bar him?"

Pace shrugged. She was putting it down to jealousy, which maybe it was.

In hindsight he knew that he should have recognized before now what was taking shape. The Bedrock lay against the John Day River, an easy ride from the confluence of that canyon-locked stream and the Columbia River. Except for the lower Bedrock, the whole immediate country was badlands, broken by watered canyons and grassy benchlands. For years this had been a natural attraction for men preferring privacy, or badly in need of it, because it was hard to penetrate, let alone take by surprise.

Now a railroad had introduced an additional factor. Building eastward from Dalles City and following the Columbia, it had reached Rowel, twelve miles north of the ranch. Once a steamboat stop, Rowel was now a helltown, graced and disgraced by all that colored a roaring railhead. The construction had brought in engineers, surveyors and hordes of construction workers. In more sinister if lesser numbers were the adventurers drawn by the excitement, and hard-bitten schemers in search of easy money.

Grading and bridge building were proceeding east from Rowel, and already there were construction camps along the right of way as far as the Umatilla. There the railroad was to split, one branch to drive north and east to meet the Northern Pacific in Montana. The other was to swing southeast to link with the Union Pacific in Utah. Each camp, and there would be many more of them, was a market for beef and for horses at prices cheaper than the legal owners would ever quote.

The whole was a setup begging for someone capable of exploiting it. Someone such as Tex Gilgen. Gilgen was handsome, arrogant, virile, and as deadly as a diamondback. The kind of man women were soft on, especially when they were as wise to the ways of the world as Arliss. . . .

She broke into his brooding to say dryly, "I'm here. Remember?"

She knew that he couldn't forget her presence if he tried. She wanted it that way, although she would never let him come to grips about things more personal than the ranch he ran largely, so far, on her money. Her aloofness was another thing he laid at Gilgen's door. She had a soft spot for the man, no matter how vague and evasive she was about him. Several times when he had come upon the two together in the saloon she ran, he had sensed undercurrents that had puzzled and annoyed him. Pace stared at her now, and she smiled back, never letting go of him and never letting him get hold of her.

He knew little about her except for what he had put together and, sometimes, guessed. He put her age at about his own, which was twenty-eight. He knew she had come from Colorado and had had money to set herself up in business in Dalles City with, surprisingly, a considerable reserve she had offered to lend him when he needed it badly. That had been several years earlier. Now, with the railroad started, she had moved her business to Rowel, which was nearer the ranch and promised to become a rival of the older town down the river.

When her sally drew nothing from him, Arliss said seriously, "You don't expect much from Hank Alper, do you?"

Pace shook his head. "He's a good enough sheriff, but no eagle. Which he'd have to be for a real good look at that country."

"They couldn't move so many horses without leaving plenty of sign."

"Sign's easy to foul and hide, given a little time. Before Alper can get out there from Dalles City, they'll have had time."

She gave him a wry smile. "So you plan something on your own hook, of course."

"Well, I aim to be up there come daylight. Before they've had much time."

"Alone?"

"That's the only way to get a look without notifying 'em in advance."

"I knew it." She moved over by the light of the lamp and picked up an embroidery ring. It was a strangely feminine pastime for a woman of her temperament, yet usually she seemed to take pleasure in it. Now it was an attempt to cover herself. It busied her hands, but it didn't hide her worry. "That's what I used to like about you, Pace. Now I'm coming to hate it. You're a born loner, and the stubbornest man I ever ran into."

"I kill my own snakes," Pace snapped.

"I know. Make sure that's what you kill."

He stared at her, then went over and threw another log on the fire, for the warming spring days were still followed by chilly nights. Straightening, he selected a cigar from the box on the mantel. Lighting it, he moved restlessly to the

11

window, trying to hide his limp as he always did when she was watching him. It was too dark to see anything but the lighted bunkhouse windows, but he remained there. So she was coming to hate what once she had liked and put her money on.

He wondered if she remembered as well as he did the night they made their commitment to one another, as limitless in one way as it was limited in the other.

He had been a drifting eighteen-year-old when he discovered the Bedrock and succumbed to the deepest love of his life. It was beautiful, a verdant jewel in a setting of tortured terrain. It had a wealth of meadow and sheltered winter range, with summer grazing all through the hills to the Blues. Water abounded, the streams joining and rejoining to tumble together into the John Day. He had known little about cattle then, but he knew what it took to make a ranch.

It had surprised him that such a treasure lay unclaimed, for stock grazing was spreading everywhere along the Columbia. He hadn't learned yet that such a country was the natural lair of a breed of men no stockman wanted near him. All he knew was that he intended to build the biggest ranch there the country would ever see. He had had himself and Bim to take care of since he was fourteen, their parents having died in an Indian raid in the Modoc region of California. Finding the Bedrock hadn't let him lay claim to it. He had spent the next two years in and around Dalles City. He had worked at any job he could find to build up his small stake, keeping Bim in school. He had visited the Bedrock as often as he could in dread of somebody's grabbing it away from him. Nobody had done so when finally he went over to the Willamette, west of the mountains, and bought a hundred head of cattle. At twenty he had become a rancher, living in a cow camp with a sixteen-year-old Bim.

Three years later they still lived in the camp. His herd had hardly more than doubled because of losses to the owl-hoot and the sales he had to make to keep going. His determination had only grown stronger in the face of that. He wanted to use the basin as fully as it deserved, and to do so he needed financial backing. So, with nothing but himself to offer for security, he had gone forth to borrow money.

Nowhere along the river or down in Portland was there a banker willing to bet on a ranch in Bedrock Basin. Its cattle and horses would be a constant temptation, they pointed out, to the rustlers, horse thieves and hungry

12

nesters already squatting on the more habitable spots. It was so isolated, there were no neighbors to call on for help. Even the sheriff preferred to forget the area as much as he could. Pace had found no arguments strong enough to overcome such objections.

He had nearly given up when, in Dalles City, he had found himself telling Arliss his troubles. She had reached there only a few months earlier by way of the stage from Kelton and had set herself up in business. He had liked to go to her place when he was in town, and they had struck up a sort of friendship. When he finished telling her of his hopes and handicaps, she had studied his face for a long and thoughtful moment.

She was making a decision, although he hadn't known that until she said, "I've got a little money I'd like to put into something promising."

He was touched as well as surprised that she had anything left over after buying her business, considering she wasn't any older than he was. "Well," he said, with an uneasy laugh, "what I had in mind is pretty steep."

"Would fifty thousand do it?"

He could only stare at her and bat his eyes. What he had in mind was a brood herd large enough to pay dividends and, at the same time, legalize his claim to the entire basin. The sum she had mentioned so casually would do that and provide help, buildings, equipment, and fencing, as well.

He asked the question he had been trying to answer to bankers. "Why would you loan *me* money like that?"

"I like a man with the gumption to bite off what you have. I'd like to help you chew it."

What she went on to tell him had convinced him that she really meant it. She had been in on a mining venture in Colorado and had made out very well. She wanted to put the money into something that nobody could take away from her. Only a small part of it had gone into the saloon, which she had bought because she wanted work to do, herself. It was doing well, but nothing like what could be made in cattle with the right kind of financing.

She didn't want it to be a loan but a partnership. She would put up the money, he the work and experience. With men to work for him he could hold his own against the owlhoot and nesters. He could pay her back gradually until their financial investments were equal. Together they would make monkeys' uncles of the stock growers who had been too timid to lay claim to the Bedrock. . . .

Pace broke off his reminiscing to see Bim coming in through the front door, looking grim and surly and more

13

than ever aloof. The day's event had shaken his tidy conclusions about that first shot from the rimrock. But he would never voice this. He couldn't without putting himself at odds with the hills.

Arliss felt the strain between the brothers, as she had now for months. She gave Bim an uneasy smile and said softly, "Hello, there."

Bim only nodded, not letting it change the set of his face. It was a handsome face, more youthful and carefree than his brother's had been at the same age. There was a softness in him that had kept Pace from taking him into the partnership, keeping him, instead, in the top job on the payroll. Bim climbed the stairs to the balcony and vanished into his room.

After a moment, Arliss said quietly, "You're losing that boy."

Pace frowned at her. "He's lost himself."

"You'd see it that way, of course."

CHAPTER 2

Within an hour after day broke over the hills, Pace had picked up the sign that had led Cob Durnbo to his death. He felt the mood of the new violence, externally in the threatening hills, but also within himself. He had reached Pistol Peak in the small hours of the morning, the night cold about him, the sky ashine with stars. At first light he had moved down to Cobble Creek and turned upstream into its canyon, remembering that Cob had said this was where the bullet had taken him.

It hadn't been long until he found a point where horses had been dropped into the canyon by way of a side stream flowing from the Pistol Peak benches. It had been impossible to tell how many riders had been on hand for the job. Once between the sheer rock walls of the canyon, the men had ridden in the drag, thus losing the prints of their own mounts. So Pace had backtracked to the open ground and returned to where the horses had first been gathered.

There, where the bunching had taken place, he had made out two sets of tracks that suggested ridden horses. He had figured from this that the riders were skilled hands, for the job had been done quickly and with a minimum of effort. For a while, then, he had sat his saddle and studied the panorama of the upper country. Cob had met the sniper's bullet on its very outskirts. He, himself, would have to probe deeply if he was to find what he was after.

So now he moved toward his goal with sunup barely at hand, an hour when no one but a sentry posted deliberately would be apt to see him. There was no need as yet to ride the sign. Once the horses were in the canyon there was no other way out except the other end. So Pace kept to the thinly timbered bench above the canyon. Twice, however, he deemed it prudent to descend through breaks in the rim to make sure he hadn't overrun his quarry.

When he reached the point where Cobble Creek picked up Sand Creek, he had to drop into the canyon to stay. The fork, itself, posed a momentary problem, for the thieves could have turned up either branch. It was a

15

chance to confuse pursuit but, to his surprise, they had gone openly up Sand Creek.

This told him more than the direction he must take, himself. If the horses were to be moved directly out and started for some distant market, they would have had to be kept on Cobble. Sand Creek led deeper into the badlands, which meant they were to be hidden in some secret recess untill it was deemed safer to move them. His property wasn't yet beyond recovery. Nor was the man who killed Cob Durnbo beyond reach.

The only one living in the immediate vicinity was a nester, Spud Stevens, on up Sand Creek where there was a pocket of meadow. Pace knew he could skirt around that sorry setup but was disinclined to do so. Stevens was bound to have seen the horses pass, although he wasn't apt to be co-operative. Pace had nothing definite against the man, though it was likely he had eaten his share of Bedrock beef. He simply disliked and despised him as one of nature's incompetents, set down on a spot so worthless nobody would contest him for it.

Even if he hadn't known the country, Pace could have told he was near the pocket from the sudden baying of the hound pack that Stevens kept. The racket they raised didn't worry him. Stevens kept them penned up except when he was running cougar or timber wolves for bounty. That was about all he did except to hunt, trap and raise a few head of stock.

The sign, Pace found, left the regular trail and curved around on the east edge of the pocket, as far from the nester setup as it could get. That hadn't been done because the horse thieves wanted to avoid being seen by the nester. It had been to keep the horses from being spooked out of control by the large-voiced dogs. Pace quit following the horse tracks and kept on along the worn trail.

Stevens' shack and tacky sheds sat by the creek on the opposite side of the pocket. The trees about were only starting to leaf out, and their bareness added to the look of desolation. Smoke rose from the shack chimney, although the hour was early for the lazy breed to be up and about. For a moment, as he rode in, a shed cut him off from the shack. When it came into view again, its door had been opened. Pace frowned. A girl stood framed there. While he wanted to see her father, he would as soon have avoided her.

One look, when he reined in before her, told him that she knew why he was there. Her small, slender body was

16

tense and her usually attractive face was dark, wary and hostile. It wasn't the horse question that brought out her antagonism. She was Bim's age, had been his first misguided passion, and she blamed Pace for breaking it up. The truth was that, while he had frowned on the attachment, it had been another wild mountain rose who towed Bim off. By comparison, Pace would have preferred this one, but he wouldn't tell her that.

He touched his hat, for he could at least respect her as a woman, and said coolly, "Morning, Wendy. Your dad around?"

She snapped him a one-word answer.

"Somewhere."

Pace would have bet that she knew exactly where that somewhere was and that it couldn't be far off. The hounds would have warned Stevens of the advent of somebody strange to them. Her father expected a grilling and was letting Wendy do the talking until he saw how things shaped up. All the nesters had to live with the outlaw element, even when they didn't work with it in secret.

Pace regarded the girl thoughtfully and said, "You'll do. What I want to know is who drove the horses that left their tracks along the far side of this pocket, yesterday afternoon or last night. Don't try to get around me, Wendy. The sign's there. They couldn't have gone through here without touching off those yapping hounds, day or night."

Stevens came around the corner of the shack, a rifle riding in the crook of his arm. He had been listening, and his eyes were flinty and aroused. He was built on the slight side like Wendy, but there they took leave of each other. Stevens' features were seamy, hard-bitten, and stained dark as an Indian's by exposure to all kinds of weather. His shaggy hair and ragged garb accented the look of a primitive.

He wasn't fool enough to deny the obvious and said readily, "Somebody went by all right, Larabee. In the night. Heard the dogs let go but never bothered to get out of bed. People go by here right along, and a man needs his sleep. If there was horses, we couldn't hear 'em because of the hounds. That answer you?"

"It's an answer."

Stevens nodded his head. "I take it they were your horses?"

"And Cob Durnbo was my man. They dry-gulched him late yesterday on Cobble Creek. But he got away and made it back to the ranch."

"Dry-gulched?" Pace turned his head to look at Wendy. That much, at least, was news to her and maybe to Stevens. Her mouth hung open, and her father's face had loosened. "He—got away?" she added.

"He's dead now."

Stevens shook his head stubbornly. "Well, we don't know anything about it. That's certain."

"If you learn anything, you better get on the right side," Pace told him. "Bedeviling my ranch is one thing for you nesters. A killing's something else. In your boots, I'd bear that in mind."

He swung his horse and rode on.

The canyon grew more rugged above the Stevens pocket. The sign continued openly, almost insolently, as before. Pace began to think the thieves had depended on speed after shooting Cob. They must have known he had got away before they could make it good. But if they didn't want to lead the law to their hideout, they would have to pull a trick out of the bag at some point.

He had passed that point before he realized he had even come near it. The sign had grown gappy due to shale and rugged places where the trail required wading in the shallow water. When he had gone by one such break and reached open going, where he should have picked up tracks again, none were to be found. He rode back to where he had last seen them and knew immediately how he had been thrown off.

The wading horses had been turned about and backtrailed in the water. That confronted him with a puzzle it would take hours to solve, if it could be done at all. With the canyon grown shallow, there were unlimited places that could be used to get out on top. The water also was shallow enough that they could have waded down past the Stevens pocket, if the nester knew about it and kept his dogs quiet. Maybe he had known and had got a laugh from the effectiveness of the trick.

Pace swung down and felt pain in his bad leg from the long period in the saddle. He made himself a smoke, needled by his vexation. He would bet that they had made this feint then gone back and continued up Cobble Creek, still in the water. Wherever they chose to leave the bottom, there would only be a short stretch of sign from the water to the bench above. It would be easy to blot, and there had been time for the disturbed earth to dry out. It would take several men many hours to check each possible exit. Even if the right one were found, every wile to deceive and delay a tracker would have been used from there on. —

18

He waited until his leg quit hurting, then swung back into the saddle. He had left word at the ranch that he would meet the sheriff at Pistol Peak at noon. Time was getting on, but before he turned back he intended to see one more nester, although one even less generous with information than Stevens had been. In the rash of quartz-mining ventures that followed the placers along the John Day, somebody had spent a lot of money at Silver Butte, which stood only a short distance back from the head of Sand Creek. Except for a shack and some sheds, the structures had been knocked apart and hauled away by nesters for their own use. Of the fizzled mine, only the adit, tailings and a lot of rusty iron remained.

Pace wasn't interested in the vestiges of somebody's lost dream but in Howie Renner, the man who had lived there the past few years with a slattern wife and a hellion of a younger sister. They weren't the kind who would choose such an isolated place to live without good reason. Yet they didn't seem to be hiding out, for they were regular visitors to Rowel. Through this, and maybe some hidden factor as well, they had become thick with Tex Gilgen.

It was only a mile from the point where the stolen horses had reversed their direction to the trail that lifted up through a steep break in the rim. Pace topped out on the timbered bench and saw the butte rearing massively above the trees. He rode steadily forward and saw with interest, as he neared the sagging house, that two men were sitting on the porch. He knew they were watching him with an intentness like his own. He was rarely in that vicinity, and if they knew anything about the horses, they were worried about why he was there now and so soon.

The house stood on a slope, and the porch floor was higher than his head when he stopped at the foot of the steps. Renner had stood up, a look of false, questioning surprise on his rotund face. For the moment he was the only one in view. Latticework screened some of the porch, causing Pace to wonder if he had ridden in on more unfriendly men than he had supposed.

Renner let his feigned expression crease into a grin. "Howdy, Larabee," he said heartily. "Don't recollect you ever done us the honor, before. Light down and rest your saddle."

Pace nodded stiffly and swung down. He trailed reins and wished he could hide the clumsiness of his leg when he climbed the flight of steps. He could never forget, when he encountered these hill people, that in his view someone among them had inflicted it on him. He came onto the porch to halt and pull up his shoulders.

There were two people there besides Renner, one the hellcat Jinx. The other was Gilgen, who sat in a chair with its back canted against the wall. Jinx was stretched out lazily on an old couch. She could have been a boy from the way she was dressed, but in no other way imaginable. She looked amused at his surprise but didn't bestir herself. She knew how he felt about her.

"Look what blew in," she said lazily.

Pace glanced at Gilgen, wondering if she was his only reason for taking up with the family, as Arliss had hinted. She would be reason enough, for she was by her own choice a torment to half the men in the country. She was the one Wendy Stevens should blame, not Bim's brother, for her falling out of favor.

Gilgen stared back at him, revealing nothing. He couldn't have been much past thirty, a well-built man, not as tall as Pace but still a man of size. He had a head of heavy, light hair, the forepart showing under the brim of the hat pushed back on his head. His face was strong, though with the strength of a powerful animal that was always uneasy but never actually afraid.

In a voice as lazy as Jinx's had been, he said, "You're a stretch from home, man. What's up?"

"His dander," Jinx offered. "What's in your craw this time, Pace Larabee? The wind blowing off us nesters and stinking up your nice basin?"

"Something like that," Pace said. "You people know Cob Durnbo?"

"Sure we know Cob." She smiled at him. It made her face strikingly attractive. "Your boys all find excuses to come to Silver Butte. Beats me why. That old mine hasn't got a thing to offer, anymore. How come you ask?"

"He was dry-gulched. Late yesterday. Down on Cobble Creek."

Her mouth dropped open. "You mean killed?"

"Shot there. And died of it."

She sat up slowly, unfolding her long body. It seemed to be news to her, yet she could play any role she chose and play it well. She and Howie were in Rowel so much, Pace had stumbled onto them there more often than in the hills. They attended many of the public dances. In a dress Jinx looked to be the prettiest, daintiest, timidest thing that ever lived. Howie, himself, cut quite a figure. While he had a fleshy face, he was only stocky and far from fat. His resemblance to Jinx was confined to his raven-black hair.

Jinx seemed really troubled when she said, "That's a pity. Cob was a real nice fella. Who could've had it in for him that bad?"

"Whoever lifted a bunch of my horses off the Pistol Peak bench." Jinx batted her eyes, which was of less interest to Pace than the glances the men exchanged. Conviction replaced his hunch that they had known that without being told. However loosely or closely, they were connected with it, and he had to smoke them on out. "I followed the sign up Sand Creek till it doubled back in the water. I've got to meet Hank Alper pretty soon and had some time to kill. Thought I'd come on up and see if you've noticed anything or anybody unusual, lately."

The mild explanation for his being there eased them somewhat. Howie shook his head. "Nope. Nothing."

"Where you meeting Alper?" Gilgen asked.

"Pistol Peak. Figured I'd get on the sign before it got too cold. But it's not the horses I'm after so much as the man who killed Cob. I've got a pretty good line on him without tracking him down."

Gilgen said with sharpened interest, "How come?"

"I talked to Cob before he died."

It was a shot in the dark, but it hit target. Howie's eyes cut uneasily to Gilgen, whose quick frown warned him to control himself. Gilgen could manage his own facial muscles but not the flow of his blood. His face had paled slightly. They knew plenty and had been worried ever since Cob got away, mortally hurt, but still able to escape them. They had admitted knowing him. So if there had been reason to fear he might have recognized one or both of them, they had felt obliged to kill him.

Pace had asked his bland question about whether they had seen anything unusual and turned to leave. Gilgen's bark stopped him.

"Where'd you talk to Durnbo?"

Pace knew he was taking his life in his hands, but it was worth the risk. "I found him on the range."

"You and who else?"

Pace felt a pulling in the muscles over his ribs. These were things Gilgen had to know. And they were dangerous questions he wouldn't ask without an idea of how to erase them. He said calmly, "Nobody, Gilgen. I come on him dying and went for help to get him home. When we got back, he was dead."

"Who you told?"

"Nobody. Why, Gilgen? You worried about somebody?"

"Curiosity," Gilgen said quickly. "Just getting it straight."

21

"Well, I don't have it straight," Jinx said suspiciously. "I think you're pulling something, Pace Larabee. If you know who done it, why waste time coming here?"

"That's a good question," Howie agreed. "If you know who done it, you know it wasn't us."

Pace stared at them, set back a notch. Maybe they weren't the ones they thought Cob had recognized. They *could* be worried about whoever it was that stood to be caught. And maybe about the ruin of plans more elaborate than had been disclosed as yet.

"I didn't say I know who it was," he returned. "I only said I've got a line on it. The rest is up to the sheriff."

He turned and left, knowing that how far he got depended on how much Jinx knew and how much she was willing to stand for.

CHAPTER 3

The shot rang sharp and loud in the upland air. Pace had expected it, moment by tense moment, ever since he came back down into the Sand Creek canyon. Withal, it was a close thing that disorganized him utterly for a split second. The sound punched into his brain even as he saw a wisp of hair fly from the mane of his horse. His muscles jerked to balance him against the shying of the horse, then he bent flat and raked his spurs. All the way he had picked out cover for himself for when it came. The best, at the moment, was a bolder nest just down from him yet seeming a mile away.

The second shot spanged off a rock on his right and went howling off through the air. The next, like an echo, connected somewhere in the hindquarters of the horse. It missed stride, kicked, and then bolted on. Pace reached the cover, knowing that without his preparedness, he would no longer be alive. He swung the horse into the boulder field, which lay at the base of the canyon wall. Dismounting, he breathed in heavy drafts of air, his eyes burning in anger.

The shots had come from the rim toward Silver Butte. They had been meant to kill him to keep him from reaching Hank Alper with the information he had pretended to possess. Knowing the vicinity intimately, it had been easy for Gilgen or Renner or both of them to cut an angle across the bench, up there, and get ahead of him.

It had been worth the gamble for it proved, at least to himself, several of his suspicions.

He jerked his rifle from the boot and crept to the edge of the rocks, moving with care. But nothing happened, then, or for long moments. He watched the rim so intently his eyes began to smart, and he knew they were taking their own wary looks, too inconspicuous up there for him to detect. It was a situation he had invited, yet he liked it less and less. He had lost track of them, but they knew exactly where he was pinned down.

Presently he grew interested in something he hadn't

noticed in his wild rush to gain cover. Just down from where the shooting took place, a narrow V-notch split the vertical wall across from his attackers. It was such that it could have been used to take the horses out of the canyon, after they came back down the creek. If this had happened, his death here could be blamed on a brush with the horse thieves, leaving the real killers in the clear.

He still could see nothing on the rim across, and the scales weighed more heavily against him with each moment that passed. He considered his chances of riding for it, flushing them in that way and fighting it out. Before he reached a decision, his horse gave sudden attention to something on down the canyon. Instantly sure that one of them had moved down below him to stop such a break, Pace crept in among the rocks on that side. It was to stare down the canyon with a checked breath. A horse and rider were coming toward him. The rider was either a boy or— it wasn't a boy. It was Wendy Stevens.

The Stevens pocket, he realized, wasn't very far on down the canyon. He had no idea of where Wendy was going or why or what to do, himself. She couldn't ride by without discovering his horse and, thus, himself. He had no doubt that the men up there on top were watching her, too. She would break up the play unless they were willing to let her in on it, on the one hand, or kill her, also, on the other.

Whatever he did, himself, she was in danger. He tried to cover her, his rifle at ready while he watched the rim above her. Apparently nobody had moved down below him. That opened a forbidding prospect. He had to warn her off, turn her back while there was still time. He was on the point of firing a shot into the air when he reconsidered.

Wendy was a hill girl. Her death would be hard to lay to stray outlaws, the way they hoped to have Cob's and maybe his own written off. It would arouse feeling among the nesters, themselves, who wouldn't believe that for a minute. If he could rely on his hunch that they wouldn't kill her, or kill him in front of her eyes, he could turn her back, make his own escape from this trap, and meet them later on better terms.

Slipping to his horse, Pace led it to the edge of the rocks and swung up, halfway expecting to feel the bite of lead. Nothing broke the deep silence of the canyon. Bent low, he dug in his spurs and went driving down toward Wendy. Much as they must have wanted to stop him, they were afraid of it. He straightened in the saddle, his arm signing Wendy to turn back. She had stopped and was staring toward him. She got the idea and whirled her horse, as though afraid of him. He swept after her. By the time she vanished around a bend in the canyon, they were beyond rifle range of the men on the rimrock.

He came around the turn to find her halted there, waiting for him. She held a rifle across her chest, but it wasn't pointed at him. She didn't look hostile the way she had that morning, although she didn't exactly look friendly. There was a little sun where she sat on her horse. It set fire to her cinnamon hair and brightened the green of her eyes.

Pace said heavily, "You don't know what you nearly got into."

"I had an idea. The hounds heard something, and I thought sure—" Wendy broke off and looked down at the ground and said no more.

"The dogs heard shooting," Pace said. "Did you aim to help me, or what?"

She looked up at him, then turned her horse and went rushing down the canyon.

He didn't try to overtake her. Nor did he contemplate going back after the men on the rim, now that he was out of their trap. It was well past noon. Alper might already have grown tired of waiting for him at Pistol Peak, and the notch he had noticed in the canyon wall held promise.

He rode on, trying to get his tangled thoughts straightened out. He was sure that Wendy had intended to help him, and he wondered why, when she hated him. Maybe it had only been for Bim's sake, since he was Bim's brother. He wished he had thanked her and still would, if he could. But when he rode through the pocket, she was nowhere in sight. So he went on toward Pistol Peak.

In spite of his worry, he found Alper waiting at the peak. Dark and burly, the man dressed like a cowhand and differed from one only by the star he wore. He sat with his back against a rock, a cigarette in his fingers. Pace swung down and winced. He had put a lot of strain on his weak leg that day.

"I started to think I'd have to go up there looking for your remains," Alper said, rising to shake hands. "Scare up anything?"

Pace debated how much to tell him. Alper had a huge county to police and wasn't inclined to consider anything but hard facts. He had closed the books on the ambush of the fall before as vagrant mischief, like everyone had but Pace, himself. Pace decided to tell the minimum until they had checked out his hunch. That would leave him free to

25

act on his own, afterward, if they didn't turn up anything substantial.

He explained how he had followed the sign nearly to the head of Sand Creek, where he discovered the ruse. And how, coming back down, he had been fired on by somebody from the rimrock and pinned down.

Since he wanted Alper's help in checking on his hunch, he altered the rest. "I'd have been there yet," he concluded, "if Wendy Stevens hadn't happened along and scared 'em off. The way it turned out, they might have tipped their hand."

"I hope so," Alper said. "I've worn my tail to a nubbin in that country. Ride up one canyon, and they scoot down another. What happened?"

"It wasn't anything that happened. I got interested in a notch where they could have taken out the horses. Maybe I was coming too close for their comfort, and they figured they'd better take care of me. They never expected something to happen to let me get away."

"It's worth a look," Alper agreed.

Pace examined the hair burn across the buttock of his horse. It was tender and would scab, but it hadn't drawn blood and hadn't hampered the horse. He swung up again and rode with Alper toward the canyon of Cobble Creek.

They had only to follow a well-worn trail and so made good time. When they entered the Sand Creek canyon they heard, faintly in the far distance, the inevitable baying of hounds. Alper said with a scowl, "That's another helpful thing about this plagued country. Them mutts of Stevens are watchdogs for everyone on above him."

"Damned near," Pace agreed. This was the main and only easy way into the hills. "If Stevens is willing to pass a warning along, he gets a chance every time."

"He might not have much choice. He's got to live with the others."

They passed through the pocket without seeing anyone, but somebody had silenced the hounds. Pace wondered if it had been Wendy. He rode on with Alper, and shortly they were at the crop of rocks. A moment later they reined in at the cleft in the wall above.

Alper looked around with interest. There was no horse sign, but that meant little, for loose rock filled the bottom of the fissure all the way up. Horses could be made to climb it without leaving many hoofprints, and what few they left could easily be swept out.

Pace glanced, a little uneasily, at the opposite rim. He saw nothing and doubted that there was anyone there, now,

26

to worry about. "Maybe you get good hunches," Alper said musingly. "Spud Stevens took me up through there one time, trailing a rustler that broke out of the county jail. If you know the way, you can make it through to the upper John Day valley quick and easy. And there's open going from there on to anywhere you're heading."

"To know the way," Pace pointed out, "you'd have to be pretty familiar with this country."

"Unless Spud Stevens was willing to guide your horse thieves, like he did me."

"Think he would?"

"Your guess is as good as mine." Alper shook his head. "But maybe it's another case of their giving him no choice. Raising a girl on the edge of an owlhoot robs a man of his independence."

"You seem to trust Stevens."

"Wouldn't call it trusting him. But I don't think he'd do anything out of the way he wasn't made to. We got pretty well acquainted, that trip. Let's see what we can scare up on top."

They started up cautiously, walking and leading their mounts. Pace's tired leg bothered him, but he led the way, carefully scanning the notch above, knowing that Alper was keeping an eye on the cut-back edge of the rim. They reached the top without trouble, to find no evidence of anyone's having been there. There was nothing in sight on the bench roundabout.

"Well, we've got an idea of where they were headed, if they come this way," Alper reflected. "It's worth riding on awhile. Sooner or later, they'll get tired of fouling sign."

Pace knew that his withholding of information was misleading the sheriff. Yet it would be easier to show than convince him of what he believed, himself. Spud Stevens knew that Alper was aware of a quick way through the badlands from this point to the upper John Day. If Stevens knew that, it was pretty sure that Gilgen and Renner knew it, too. They wouldn't have taken or sent the horses out that way this soon.

"I dunno, sheriff." Pace shook his head. "Things got hotter than they expected. Too hot for them to leave the badlands till they really have to. It would be safer for them to play hide-and-seek, right here, awhile."

Alper gave him a glum eye. "To play that game with 'em, I'd need half the country for a posse."

"Not if we narrow down the area to comb. I think we can. Nobody knows this country like Stevens does. If

27

they're forcing him to help, they could hold him responsible for keeping the critters hidden awhile."

"If they're threatening him or his girl," Alper said, with a shake of the head, "he'd never give *me* any help."

"No," Pace agreed. "But something you said stuck in my mind. About his hounds being an early warning. I think those horses were brought up this notch to the bench. It's my guess they're still somewhere with easy access to it and to water. That narrows it plenty, and there's one more thing. They've got to be where Spud can reach them quick, if they have to be moved."

Still skeptical, Alper said, "Somebody went to a lot of trouble to set up a system like that."

"Because somebody figures to whittle on me till I'm bled white," Pace said. "We're getting ready to bring the herd up to summer. So soon it'll be steers, too. There's plenty of market in the construction camps, all the way up the river."

Alper took a tobacco plug from his pocket, bit off a chew and settled it in his cheek. He nodded, at last. "You don't comfort me with ideas like that. But they're worth checking on. Not starting from here, though. Them hounds have already told everyone in earshot that we're around. We'd best go down, like we were leaving, and find another way to come back."

CHAPTER 4

Once more their passage through the Stevens pocket was heralded by the hounds, which nobody silenced, suggesting that now no one was home. The annoying baying didn't fade out until Pace and Alper were nearly down to the Cobble Creek fork. There they turned back into the badlands, for Cobble angled away, with the bench above widening steadily to the south. By going in that way they could keep out of earshot of the dogs, but it was a rough route. Cobble Canyon was wider than the other, but above the fork there were stretches where the water washed against the very walls.

This, with other obstacles, made it improbable that this approach to the upper country was guarded, yet they took each visible stretch of the canyon with care. The walls pinched in, rapids and rocks confronted them, with pools that rose belly-deep on their horses. Pace was wondering if they would ever make it out on top.

A chip of dry flat appeared abruptly on the right side. It was covered by coarse sand and fragmented rock fallen from the wall above, with about a ten-foot break in the wall directly behind. Horse tracks and droppings littered the sand to the edge of the water. Horses in numbers came there regularly to drink. The riders reined in, looking around and at each other.

"We're back and not too far above the Stevens pocket," Pace said quietly. "And Spud don't own that many horses."

"He sure don't," Alper agreed. He glanced on up the canyon. "I wonder if there's a place farther on where I could get up, while you go up here."

"Why don't you see?" Pace suggested. "If there isn't, come back and follow me up this way. You'd be an ace in the hole, if I run into trouble up there."

"All right. And don't you start trouble till you know where I am."

Pace nodded and crossed the sand, his horse dripping water. The break looked black and forbidding. He entered, momentarily blinded by the darkness, the only light he

29

could see being at the top and deep in the bench. But his horse moved without difficulty, and presently Pace could see that the bottom was carpeted with finely fractured rock, indicating that there had been considerable traffic here over the years. He rode almost to the top, then stopped and dismounted. He nearly fell as his weight came down on his bad leg; he had pushed too hard this day. Carrying his rifle, he crept on until he could barely see out across the bench.

The first thing he spotted was his horses. He had been so sure of it that this gave him no surprise. They were out from him, grazing or standing about, and apparently were allowed to go and come to the creek as they chose. The men guarding them weren't worried about their escaping down the creek, nor had they been concerned about some outsider's showing up that way. They must have posted themselves where they could keep an eye on the bench, itself. Their probable location was suggested by a belt of scrub pine that screened off the bench to the south and west. The place was made to order for the systematic stealing he had described to Alper.

Pace walked on up, gaining elevation for a backward look at the rim. It was brushier than the open ground, with no setback to indicate a break where Alper could climb out of the canyon. He studied the rim brush and decided that he could ride through it as safely as he could walk. He went down and brought up his horse.

Mounted, he made the brush without causing any kind of disturbance. But he hadn't ridden two hundred yards toward the pines when everything blew apart. In his first confusion, he thought it was Stevens' hound pack that had cut loose. But the pocket was far away, and the sudden commotion was right at hand. And, he soon realized, it was made by only one dog. Stevens had loaned or been forced to lend them one of his hounds. Pace frowned worriedly, for it offset the luck they had had in finding this approach to the hideout.

At least the bugling creature would have rattled the guards as much as it had him. Pace raked his spurs, caution no longer helpful. The sentry or sentries would have been on the far side of the pines, but the hound had pointed him. He was still short of the trees when the first challenge came on this side, the sharp percussion of a rifleshot. Two more followed before his horse swept in among the trees, toward the rim from whoever had shot at him.

The scrub belt wasn't wide, there was little undergrowth,

30

and he had nothing but the trunks of the trees to screen him. A hasty scanning of the rim on the far side showed no place where Alper could have ascended. That was to the good, for he would have to come in the way Pace had himself and would be on the other side of the scrub from where Pace found himself. Alper couldn't have helped hearing the commotion and would make his own moves forewarned.

Pace swung down, steadied himself and left his mount, which was too easy to spot. Forted behind the largest tree he found, at a distance of some fifty feet from the horse, he studied the open spaces under the crowns of the trees. The man or men who had shot at him had lost him, momentarily, and he failed to locate them. The hound still yammered furiously and might be pointing him. He saw no sign of saddle horses, but there would be one or more in there somewhere.

Then he saw movement, off to his left, that nearly impelled him to shoot. He waited in grim patience, never shifting his gaze from the spot. A man looked out cautiously from behind a tree. He seemed to have caught a glimpse of the Bedrock horse and was directing his attention that way. Pace had never seen him before, a man with the dark, sharp look of a wolf. He could have killed him, but the fellow would be worthless dead and might be of some use if captured.

His rifle at ready, the man was all wariness while he slid over behind a nearby tree, which was closer to the Bedrock horse. There he made a hand sign, and another man of the same cut stepped out from behind a tree beyond. They moved closer to each other, then were both hidden while they called back and forth. The hound was taking longer between howls but still kept Pace from making out what they said.

He used the interval to make a short, careful move of his own, hoping to get between them and their mounts before he disclosed his position. Somewhat to his surprise he got away with it and failed to bring another spasm from the hound. He risked another move and was his own undoing. The foot of his bad leg dragged on something that sent him crashing down. A shot kicked leaf mold and litter in his face almost before he recovered his wits. He scrambled on to his objective, making it just as another near-miss threw up trash.

He was between them and where he guessed their mounts to be, with them between him and his own. They liked that even less than he did and peppered the ground on both

31

sides of his tree. Flattened behind it, he waited through what seemed an hour, wincing each time a bullet tore bark or threw up litter. But he had to wait for Alper.

When the hound went into another and unbroken frenzy, it sent excitement coursing through him. Alper had at last got close enough for the dog to pick him up. Gambling that the two men were concentrating on the new disturbance, Pace lifted his rifle and stepped out. Nothing happened. They knew they were bracketed, and their looks didn't suggest they would let themselves be taken without a fight.

From his changed position, he couldn't be sure which trees shielded the two from his side. He picked a prospect, fired, and saw bark go flying. He shot again just as another shot cracked out beyond them. It flushed them, and they came out shooting, moving fast. Pace picked a pair of legs, fired at them, and saw their owner spill headlong. Other shots rang out, and when he wheeled he saw the second man jerk upright. He fell backward, his rifle flying from loosened fingers. Pace ran forward just as Alper came bounding through the trees on beyond them.

There was no fight left in the pair. The one on his back was stocky, with a whiskery face and ragged hair. The one with the bleeding leg was thin, gawky and plenty scared. He hadn't known until he saw Alper's star that he was in the hands of the law.

"What's this all about, sheriff?" he said, in a whining voice. "We figured you for hoss thieves."

"Don't give me that," Alper snorted. "When you were holding stolen horses, yourselves."

"They stolen?" The man acted surprised. "We was just hired to guard 'em. The man said this country's full of bad eggs."

Alper knew he was lying and said with disdain, "We'll see how long you stick to that after I get you to jail."

"You won't lock this one up," Pace said. He had walked over to the other man. "He's dead."

"Won't have to try him, either," Alper said grimly.

Pace found the sheriff's horse a short distance beyond his own and brought both back. Alper had gathered the gunmen's rifles. He had handcuffed the man they had taken alive and done a rough job of tying up his bleeding thigh. The still noisy hound led them to the outlaw camp and horses, west of where the fight had taken place. The unhappy dog was tied there to a tree. Alper turned it loose and it went streaking off over the bench toward the pocket.

Pace felt like he had a ton of bricks on his back and,

with the tension leaving him, his knee throbbed. He rolled a cigarette while Alper bit a chew off his plug.

Nodding toward the receding dog, Alper said, "You want to bring an aiding and abetting charge against Stevens?"

Pace shook his head. "You sold me on the idea that he couldn't help himself. I ought to say he can't. I got my horses back, but we haven't broke it up. Maybe we haven't even nailed the man who killed Cob Durnbo."

Alper frowned at him. As far as he was concerned, the case had been cleaned up, the horses recovered and the thieves dealt with. "What makes you say that?" he asked grumpily.

"I think Cob recognized somebody, and I doubt that he ever laid eyes on this pair. I doubt that you'll sweat much out of your prisoner. So it'd be smart to leave Stevens alone. We're onto this stash hole, but he knows all kinds of *them,* and ways to get out of the badlands in any direction, I'd guess. So they'll keep using him, if we leave him be. And maybe next time we'll get farther."

Alper thought it over, then nodded his head.

They tied the dead man onto one of the horses found at the camp and helped the injured prisoner to mount. Alper waited with his charges while Pace rounded in his own horses and got them started down the canyon-walled trail to Cobble Creek. That way was shorter and safer, under the circumstances. If the prisoner knew anything about the operation, the men behind him wouldn't want him to leave the country alive.

The day was nearly gone when they came down on the Pistol Peak bench, and it was full dark when they reached ranch headquarters. Alper wanted to go on to Rowel at once. There was a town jail there, a doctor, and train service to Dalles City. He would hold the inquest there, for a couple of ranch hands had taken Durnbo's body in that day in a buckboard. Pace insisted that he wait long enough to eat a meal at the cookshack. He promised to be on hand for the inquest, then lent Alper a couple of men to make sure nothing happened to the prisoner on the ride to Rowel.

Pace himself had eaten nothing since the evening before and was too worn-out to be really hungry, but he made himself eat with Alper. Once he had seen the sheriff off, he went to the big house to find Arliss still on the ranch and waiting for him. She had already learned the essentials from the activity but wanted to know more about it. He felt that, as her partner, he could and should tell her more

33

than he had been willing to tell Alper. It had a strangely disturbing effect on her.

"Maybe you're right." She seemed extremely reluctant to admit it. Her cheeks were pale, and there was a shocked concern in her eyes that she couldn't conceal. She hesitated a moment in confusion, then added, "You don't like Tex Gilgen. But he really hates you."

"Why?" Pace asked, surprised.

She looked away from him. "For one thing, I'm your partner. And I spend a lot of time out here."

"That's your business, not his."

"He doesn't think it's my own business."

"He's in love with you?"

"He was."

Pace studied her troubled face. "Was? You've been my partner longer than he's been around here."

"I know. I—" She broke off, then said in a rush, "If you'll excuse me, I'll go to bed. I have a headache. But I wanted to make sure you're all right."

"Sure. Go ahead."

He watched her climb the stairs and hurry along the balcony to her room, knowing she was only trying to escape more questions. It left him more puzzled than before. Before he could pick at it, the door opened, and Bim came in from outdoors.

They had spoken to each other only briefly during the excitement aroused by the returned horses, the sheriff, dead man and prisoner. When Bim hooked his hat on the rack by the door and turned, there was a look on his face that gave Pace a small shock. He thought that, like Arliss, Bim was going on up to his room to avoid him. But he stopped short of the stairway, turned and stared at Pace.

"You had a man killed yesterday," he said heavily. "Oldtimer here. Killed helping you get rich and big and a man to be envied. The boys set up with him, last night. So did I. You never come near him, once you know why he got killed. Off you went into the hills to get back your horses."

Pace stared back at him. Bim had never talked to him like that before, and his eyes showed he had more to say if given the chance. Pace wondered if he had ever really known the boy and how he looked to him. "You think they're the reason I went up there?" he asked.

"You brought 'em back, didn't you?"

"Incidentally. I went up there to find out who killed Cob. I think I did. I'll prove and square it for him. I think that's as good as setting up with him."

34

"Then who done it?"

"I'm not ready to say."

"There you are." Bim lifted his shoulders. "The big loner. Showing the trash up there that they better not fool with Pace Larabee."

Pace blinked at him. There had been no vain arrogance in what he had done, at least none had been intended. It was just his way to take care of things himself. He had been doing it much of his life and even more of Bim's, although he hesitated to remind Bim of it. He could only take cover by taking the offensive.

"So you admit there's trash up there," he said in mock surprise.

"They're not all trash."

"Well—not if they're pretty."

"See here." Bim's eyes blazed with anger he could no longer moderate. "I let you badger me out of seeing Wendy Stevens, and now she despises me for being that spineless. No more of that. I've paid off whatever I owed you for raising me. I don't aim to let you run any more of my life."

"What's that got to do with me being a big loner? That seems to be what's touched you off."

"It's got everything to do with it. You're bigger than anybody, and so damned good you don't even need to belong to the human race."

"That's news to me," Pace said.

"Time you heard it, and a few other things. You can't trust the judgment of anybody else, or tolerate anybody who isn't cut to your pattern, or depend on anybody else to solve what are *your* problems. Like, for instance, what I do with my life."

Pace scowled. If there was any truth in that, it was because he had been made that way. "You're telling me to let you have your head with Jinx Renner. A lot of men have been trying to rope that filly. If you're the one that does it, you'll be sorry."

"You don't know her. I do."

"I hope you do," Pace said heavily. "I seen her today at Silver Butte. Tex Gilgen was there. I let on that Cob recognized one of the horse thieves and lived long enough to tell me. Nobody but me. They knew I was about to meet the sheriff. And I damned near got shot again on my way down from there."

Bim's mouth dropped open. "You think *they* were in on it?"

"Don't be a bigger fool than nature turned out."

"Tex Gilgen could be," Bim said harshly. "I don't like

35

him a little bit, myself. But not Jinx or Howie or any of
the other nesters. Man, I'm starting to think what they
all do. You're *looking* for an excuse to run 'em out."
Bim wheeled and stomped up the stairs.

CHAPTER 5

From where he stood on Windy Point, Pace could see the sprawled and ugly aggregation of men and the works of men, that called itself Rowel City, which lay below him by the river. His interest, at the moment, was in the shining iron of the Oregon, Washington Railroad & Navigation Company track, imbedded on the Oregon shore and coming east from Dalles City. The creeping rails were making tremendous changes, and while this excited him, it depressed him, too.

Below, at the old landing, lay the *D. S. Baker,* still competing for inland trade since no rails ran, as yet, east of Rowel or westward beyond Dalles City. But she was doomed and her sister, the handsome *Harvest Queen,* had already given up the struggle and gone down over the rapids at high water to work on the lower river. Pace thought of other boats that, in his own time, had plied the Columbia above the old Dalles City-Deschutes portage railroad. Most of them had been driven upriver and beyond the reach of the railroad, the *John Gates, Annie Faxon, Almota,* and many others. Soon they would all be gone, he thought. Their solemn, leisured whistling, rolling off the rock cliffs, would be replaced by the rushing racket of the steamcars.

It was a comfort to know that the cars could never change the rugged, natural grandeur of the region. His roving gaze swept over the river to the far, blunt cliffs and the bare, rolling hills above them. Westward, the towering green of the Cascades slowly dissolved in the twilight. Southward lay the benches and canyons enfolding Bedrock Basin, his own piece of the country. If, he thought grimly, he could hold onto it. The inquest held that afternoon had pointed the direction the grand jury would take, the trial jury, and events in the Bedrock, itself.

He turned with impatience and started back down the trail to the town. After the inquest was over, he had headed home and then changed his mind. All the men who had seen Cob Durnbo die had come in with him. This included

37

Bim. While they hadn't attended the inquest, Jinx Renner, her brother, and Tex Gilgen were also in town. The day was Saturday, and Rowel held a public dance on that night. This had probably drawn Jinx. If the inquest hadn't been an attraction to Howie and Gilgen, its outcome must have been a deep relief to them.

Pace came onto the main street of the town, whose smoky lamps had been lighted for the night. It was an elongated street and town, pushed by the river, main track, sidings and huge stockpiles against the cliffs cut by erosion into the bench above. He felt like a stranger now, for men wholly strange to the region thronged the place, drowning out the native element. He continued on along the boardwalk, thinking of dropping in to see Arliss. She had returned to town with them, but he hadn't seen her since the inquest.

The purpose of the proceedings had been to establish the fact of Cob Durnbo's death, examine the circumstances, and render an opinion as to the person or persons responsible. There had been several men to attest that Cob had died of a gunshot wound. The rest depended on Pace's testimony and that of the sheriff. Viewed factually, it had wrapped up handily in a finding that Cob had met his death at the hands of Purdy Ehrman, which the prisoner called himself, and one George Munson, deceased, while they were engaged in an attempt to steal horses from Bedrock Ranch.

Pace, in his testimony, had stated the objective fact that he, himself, had been fired on several times by someone on the west rim of Sand Creek Canyon. But there was nothing to show that the thieves, guarding against the discovery of their hideout, hadn't themselves crossed the canyon before attacking him. Purdy Ehrman offered no information, resigned to the probability that, others in it or not, he would stand trial for murder and be hanged.

Pace saw none of his own men among the hundreds thronging the street. He doubted that he would see many of them before Monday morning, for a railhead held many covert allures for men just in from the big lonesome. He had his supper and bought a cigar, still uncertain about seeing Arliss before he went home. He hadn't tried to question her again. But she had told him, in effect, that she and Gilgen had known each other elsewhere and that Gilgen had been in love with her. He wished he could persuade her that she owed him more help than that.

She called her saloon the Fandango, and it was one of the few in town without girls. This cost her most of the

38

construction trade, but that seemed to suit her. When he reached the door, he turned in automatically.

Compared to the honky-tonks and deadfalls, the Fandango's atmosphere was quiet and relaxed. The fixtures and furnishings were expensive and in good taste. Well-dressed men, some from the railroad but more from the town and drawn for business reasons to the town, stood at the bar. Others of the same ilk sat at card tables or were gathered about the pool tables at the deep end of the room.

Usually Arliss lent her presence in the evening, but she wasn't in evidence. Pace knew where to look, left the place, and climbed the outside stairs to her living quarters and rapped on her door. She seemed to have expected him, for her only greeting was a faint smile while she stepped back for him to come in.

"I guess you heard how it come out," he said tiredly.

She nodded. "About as expected."

"I guess so. The admissible evidence stacked up like a rick of cordwood."

Arliss motioned him to sit down, reoccupied her chair and picked up her embroidery ring. She always seemed so different here, to the way she seemed at the ranch. Now a form-fitting gown and piled-up hair style made her coolly and strikingly beautiful, putting her so far out of reach it was no wonder she had never encouraged his attentions.

He dropped his hat on a chair, sat down where he could look at her, relit his cigar, and let fire at her. "Were you, in turn," he asked, "in love with Tex Gilgen?"

She lowered the needlework into her lap and lifted startled eyes. "I thought you got the idea. I don't want to talk about that."

"But I want to."

She whipped him a look so keen and dark, he almost wished he hadn't reopened the subject. "So I see. Why?"

"Whatever he was and you were, I take it he hates you now like you said he hates me. Otherwise I don't see how he could set out to steal from a ranch set up mostly on your money."

"All right. He hates me now. I tried to get away from him and hide and did, until he found me here. Pace, I've told you enough to help you protect yourself and our interests. Let it go at that. Please?"

"Not when you've thrown more shadow than light. I mean about us, Arliss. Why we can be partners and nothing else."

She sighed. "You're right. I hoped I'd never have to

tell you. I was and, legally, I still am Tex Gilgen's wife."

Pace felt like something had shaken the whole building. She wasn't looking at him, and her cheeks were drained, her mouth trembling. He said feebly, "Where was this?"

"Blackhawk. He was unfaithful. To make matters worse, he was cruel. I couldn't stand it any longer. A friend offered me a chance to go in on the venture I told you about. It paid off, and I ran away. Tex learned of the money I'd made, but it took him a while to run me down."

"Which was he after," Pace asked. "You or the money?"

"Mostly the money. It's harder to come by than women, at least for him. When he found out it wasn't in the form of money, anymore, but in something he couldn't take away from me, he swore he'd get it another way. That's what he's trying to do."

Pace could only watch her with bleak eyes. Queerly, his strongest reaction, at the moment, was against the fact that she was, and had been through their acquaintance, a married woman.

He said roughly, "Divorce him."

"That wouldn't stop him."

"It would free you."

"What for?"

"You and me."

She shook her head. "No, Pace. It can't ever be you and me."

"You don't care?"

"I don't dare. Oh, please. I've told you more than you needed to know." She looked up at him with moist eyes. "Go now?"

Pace was hardly aware of moving down the stairs to the street. Never had he felt so direct, so driving a desire for her, or been so aware of her eyes, her mouth, the curves of her body. Gilgen had known all that, and he wanted to kill Gilgen.

As Gilgen wanted to kill him, not knowing how little he had had of Arliss personally? Did he owe the knee that reminded itself to him as he tramped along the sidewalk to that? Yet maybe that first shot in this war had had a more practical purpose. With him out of the way, the Bedrock would be far easier to take over. Bim, his heir, was already half-undermined by his feelings for the nesters. Arliss was still Gilgen's legal wife, affording a basis for the man's moving in.

Pace grew aware of music coming from down the street and remembered the dance. The sound was punctuated with the mass stamping of feet, with bursts of laughter and high-spirited shouts. Bim would be there, and some of the other men from the Bedrock. Pace decided to see Bim before he left town and tell him to make sure they were all on the ranch and able to work Monday morning. He crossed the street and walked down to the double-doored entrance of the dance hall.

Men were bunched outside on the steps and sidewalk. Most of them had their coats off and were out there to cool off from whirling the girls and women. Bottles were passing hand to hand, jokes and amiable insults with them. Pace nodded to a few he knew, then pushed through and went up into the hall.

A whirlpool of humanity crowded the soap-slickened floor. The set dance that had caused the racket had given way by then to a twosome. He watched a spirited two-step to its end without seeing Bim. The dance stopped, and the couples kept walking around the floor, waiting for the music to strike up again. When it did, Pace saw Jinx Renner. She had emerged from somewhere, not with Bim but with Gilgen. It was a tag waltz, for stags began to cut in from the sidelines. A lot of them were watching Jinx, stunning with neatly arranged hair and in a pretty dress, but nobody dared to cut in on Gilgen.

Pace watched the two swing toward him on the edge of the floor. They were good dancers, and both liked being out where they could be seen by the wallflowers. Then Gilgen saw him. His face didn't change except for a look of mockery that ghosted there for a second. That was enough. Pace forgot his bad leg, stepped out as they passed, and dropped his hand on Gilgen's shoulder.

They stopped, Gilgen startled out of his smiling geniality. Jinx's eyes widened, but she looked amused. Pace supposed she wouldn't mind a tangle over her with much of the town looking on.

Meeting Gilgen's now hostile eyes, Pace said easily, "Mind?"

"Why—not at all."

Gilgen stepped back, mockery in his eyes again and in his elaborate bow. He turned and walked off the floor. Jinx looked up at Pace. Something in her expression reminded him that, after the nimble Gilgen, he would put on a pretty poor dancing exhibition for the spectators. She wasn't going to let him out of it. She stepped closer, and he swung her onto the floor. Every reserve of his will went into controlling his bad knee. He managed it pretty well.

"I never expected to wind up in *your* arms," Jinx mur-

41

mured. "Must've made a bigger hit than I thought, the other day."

"I'll do the talking," Pace snapped.

"Well, shut my big mouth. Here? Or out under the stars?" Her expression changed, and she said, "Hey. You do real well. I'm glad."

"Why?"

"I didn't like what happened to you. Always thought you could get over it, if you'd stop using it to nurse your grudge against us nesters. What did you want to talk about?"

"Bim." He was angry enough to be reckless. "If you don't stop leading him on, I'm going to forget you're a woman."

She laughed. "What makes you think you could, Pace, if he can't?"

Pace wished he hadn't said that. If she taunted Bim with it, it would be the last he saw of his brother. He fell silent, hoping somebody would cut in. But he seemed to have inspired the same timidity about that, that the stags had shown toward Gilgen.

Jinx looked up at him. "If you've had your say, I'll have mine. I know Bim better than you do. And he knows *you* better than you do. What a bigheaded, pigheaded would-be cattle king you are, for instance." The music stopped, and she smiled sweetly. "If you want to hear the rest, you'll have to dance with me again."

Pace pinched his lips and walked beside her, trying to hide his limp and succeeding better than he ever had before. "Bim tell you all that?" he said heavily. "Or you him?"

"They were my conclusions, but he's reached them, too, now."

"I sure appreciate your meddling."

"Who's a meddler?" she said with a hoot.

The music struck up. She lifted her arms, came into his, and fell silent while they joined the dancers.

It was a long moment before Pace said, "When it comes to questions, I've got a few. Did you know why I threw such a scare into Gilgen and Howie, the other day at Silver Butte? That they tried to kill me on my way down from there? You know that Gilgen's declared war on the Bedrock, and why?"

She glanced up with widened eyes, and at the same moment a hand fell on his shoulder. Pace turned his head to see Bim standing there, his face truculent and dark with suspicion. He stopped and thought that Jinx caught her own breath before she flashed Bim her wicked smile.

She shook her head reprovingly. "It's not a tag dance, Bimbo. And I'm having such a nice talk with your brother."

Pace stared at her, dismayed and furious. Her eyes flicked to his, less amused now than deadly. Bim looked at them both in disbelief, then wheeled and strode off the floor. She couldn't have subjected him to a greater humiliation, and it could only have been to drive in the wedge irrevocably.

Jinx lifted her arms again, still wearing that maddening smile. He said raggedly, "That's something else you'll be sorry for," and turned and hurried after his brother. But Bim could walk faster than he could and had vanished into the crowd.

Pace was hurrying down the steps to the street when he came face to face with Gilgen, returning to the hall from some saloon. There was a flush in the man's face, an increased recklessness in his eyes.

Gilgen said with a thin grin, "She's a hard gal to hold onto, ain't she?"

Pace halted, despairing of overtaking Bim, even if it would do any good. "You talking about Jinx?" he asked.

"Who else?"

"Didn't know but what you meant your old friend from Blackhawk."

Gilgen sucked in his breath. He glanced around uneasily. They were the only ones on the steps, at the moment, and no one on the walk below was paying attention. "So she told you," he muttered.

"Finally. She didn't seem proud of it."

"I bet she never told you all of it."

"She told enough. Gilgen, don't count yourself too lucky in the way things come out, today. That pair's guilty. But somebody was with 'em that Cob Durnbo recognized. Remember?"

Pace had brought that up on a hunch, but Gilgen's eyes went bleak. "What's that mean to me?"

"What it meant to you at Silver Butte."

"If you think it was me," Gilgen demanded, "why didn't you tell Alper?"

"I know it was you or Howie Renner. And I'd rather prove than tell it."

The hatred Arliss had warned of, flooded Gilgen's eyes. "If you live long enough," he retorted.

CHAPTER 6

It was always hard to work the breaks where the hills piled against Baldy Slope. So Pace had assigned himself to that section, with Spike Munson helping him. It had been frosty that morning, when the crew scattered in a circular sweep from the first setting of the calf roundup. By eight o'clock the June sun had burned off the frost and warmed the air until Pace had shucked his coat and tied it to his saddle. His horse was showing sweat because it was hard on horses as well as riders to work that kind of country. All morning, so far, he had cleaned out pockets and herded what he gathered toward the branding fires.

The first warming days after the murder had seen the dry bunch moved off winter range in the lower basin. Now the whole herd was settled, for better or worse, on the grassy benches in the upcountry, next to the nesters and the owlhoot. Baldy was the easternmost range and less exposed to the new danger than Bear Prairie and Pistol Peak, the latter being the point where the roundup would end. But Baldy had to be worked while, at the same time, a careful watch was maintained against rustlers on the more exposed ranges westward. This had forced Pace to put on even more extra help and, even so, he was spread thin. So far there had been no trouble, but he didn't think for a minute that there wasn't plenty of it coming.

He was resting his horse as well as his aching knee when he saw Bim riding up the open slant toward him and wondered if some of it had shown up. He had had a hard time talking Bim into staying on the ranch and in his job. Bim was still inturned and sullen, but he had stayed away from Jinx Renner since that night at the Rowel Dance Hall. Instead of bringing about the split she must have hoped for, Jinx had lost her hold on Bim by humiliating him. Yet Pace found little satisfaction in that. His own hold was gone. Bim was staying on only because he had finally been convinced that the Bedrock was in a fight for its life. Once that was settled—Pace shook his

44

head, sorrowful and curious as to what was bringing Bim to him when usually he avoided contact like poison.

He rolled a cigarette and waited. There was no excitement in Bim's eyes when he came on up the slope, nothing but the chilly stand-offishness of recent weeks. Yet what he said was electrifying.

"Froggy Jorgensen just seen a nester who'd been down to Rowel. Word there is that Purdy Ehrman was shot and killed. Through a window. Right in his own cell in the county jail."

For a moment Pace could only blink at him. Alper had taken Ehrman on to Dalles City and had been holding him for the next session of the grand jury and circuit court. "Well, what do you make of it?" he asked.

"What you do," Bim said. "Somebody didn't trust him to hold up in front of the grand jury."

"Somebody sure didn't." Pace hesitated. Yet he couldn't resist the chance to point out how right he had been. He plunged ahead. "I hope it persuades you you were playing with rattlesnakes when you fooled around in the hills."

Bim frowned, his cheeks coloring. Then he got hold of himself and said doggedly, "I still say it's not the nesters. I conceded you Tex Gilgen. Maybe I'd concede Howie Renner. He likes you about the way you like him. But not Jinx. Not Spud Stevens and not Wendy. Nor any of the other nesters, whatever they think of Bedrock Ranch."

"All right." Pace was glad to drop it at that.

A silence hung between them. Bim had made his report, and there was nothing left to talk about. The truth was that they weren't brothers any longer, Pace thought, while he watched Bim wheel his horse and ride away. They were boss and hired hand, with even that bond frayed, and it came to him that maybe Bim was right. Maybe that was all he had let them be for a long while.

He combed pockets for a couple more hours. When he and Munson split that morning, Munson had ridden west for some distance and then begun to work back. It was midmorning when they came back together. That was all the flushing they would do in the forenoon circle. Thereafter they worked together, zigzagging behind the cattle and calves already popped from the pockets. These had fallen to grazing again as soon as they came out on the open slope. Now they were tightened and moved slowly in toward the branding camp.

The sun stood high when the first lot came together on the holding ground near the chuck wagon and fires. A couple of riders stayed with the cattle, while the others rode in to the wagon to eat. Bim was at the fires. Washing up at the wagon, Pace thought again about having changed, somewhere along the way, from brother to boss. He realized that even on the roundup he really ran things, himself, in spite of Bim's title. Yet he still felt it had to be that way. Bim was popular with the men and put too high a value on their friendship, which made him soft with them. On top of that, it was no year to let him handle the roundup by himself, when he was equally soft and gullible with the nesters.

As fast as they finished eating, the men saddled fresh horses. Some had to let the punchers on herd come in to eat. Others got ready to go out on the afternoon gather. Pace sent a man out in his place and worked through the afternoon at the branding fires, liking to keep an eye on every aspect of the work. That at the fires was noisy, dirty, sweating, and went on without a break through the long afternoon. By the time the morning gather was worked, he could see clouds of dust rising in the distance all about. The incoming gather would be worked the next forenoon, and so on to the end of roundup. Then would come the summer work and, in the fall, the beef gather and market drives.

Pace regarded that drawn-out, grueling prospect with dread for the first time. Much of the northwest range was too broken and isolated for large roundup associations, each outfit doing its own. Once he had liked that independence. Now it made him feel alone and vulnerable in so many ways.

The sun hung on the western rims when work was finally knocked off. Elvek, the cook, served the last meal of the day. The wrangler picketed the night horses near camp. The rest of the *remuda* was moved far enough away to graze, hobbled, without bothering the bunched cattle. The temperature sank with the sun, and the men built up the campfire. A harmonica came out of somebody's pocket, a deck of cards appeared. These amusements wouldn't hold sway very long, Pace knew. The men were dead-beat, and they all had night herd ahead.

He turned in with the first of them, for his knee was giving him fits. He seemed barely to have fallen asleep when a quiet voice awakened him. He sat up quickly to see Swede O'Brien hunkered above him.

"Something's got the critters spooky," O'Brien whispered. "Bim's out there. He figured I better come in and tell you."

Pace nodded, frowning, and the puncher faded into the night. Dressing was only a matter of pulling on his boots

46

and putting on his hat, so he soon had a horse off picket. Bunched cattle were always nervous, he knew, particularly at the start of the season when they weren't used to being pushed. They were never sound sleepers, except in the hours before midnight, and from then until daylight they would be up and down. Some would stray off the bedground unless they were kept rounded in. But it would have to be more than that for Bim to have sent in for him.

By the time he reached the herd, Pace knew from the stars that it was around two in the morning. The whole bunch was on its feet. Low, throaty rumbling told him they were feeling something more than the usual night anxiety. Bim had joined the two men on herd to help hold back the bobblers. Pace rode counterwise, the quickest way to find him. When they met, they pulled off a short distance, for even talk could have an explosive effect on jumpy cattle.

"Don't know what got into 'em," Bim said quietly. He had been out since the previous change of guard, he said, when the riders coming off herd had told him about this. None of the usual disturbants were present. They hadn't been having the sticky weather that could build up static electricity, to which steers' horns were sensitive. "I hated to rob the boys of their sleep, putting them all on herd at once. Figured I better see what you think of it."

Pace stared at him through the starshine, puzzled as to whether Bim didn't know what to do or was afraid to act on his own hook. "Could be they smell a timber wolf."

"I thought of that," Bim said. "It don't seem likely. Spud Stevens' bounty hunting has kept them cleaned out, the last few years."

"A new pair could have drifted in."

"Maybe. You want me to rouse the other boys?"

Pace shook his head. He was worried, too, but a hard day's work for all of them lay ahead, a factor that had restrained Bim, too. "I'll stay. The four of us can handle 'em."

They fell into place, scattered at equal distances as they rode quietly around the bedground. Whatever bothered the animals, it had only made them wary and restless, as yet, without really spooking them. That strengthened Pace's suspicion of a timber wolf or a pair of them lurking near, hungry for the young calves. The riders would keep them from coming any nearer. He would have a look after daylight, and if he found wolf sign he would have a new worry. The predators would have to be destroyed, or there would be trouble from that source all summer, too.

47

It was about an hour later when he learned how badly and how incompletely he had judged the situation. He was on the upslope side of the herd when he heard the first racket. It came from toward the hills but from someplace nearer. He swiveled in the saddle to see a horse come out of a draw and continue on at a thundering gait, heading straight toward him and the cattle. Something bounded and soared and slatted behind it, making even more noise than the pounding hoofs.

The kitelike object told him instantly that human meddling was involved. He jerked his rifle from the boot and drove in his spurs. The steers were already surging and trying to mill. But they might hold if he could turn away the awesome apparition bearing down. He drove headlong at the racing horse, which was in a panic itself because of the thing tied to its tail. He knew by then that this was a dried cowhide, stiff as a board. It was an old trick for stampeding cattle.

The hide drummed the ground and bounced in the air, and the mindless creature towing it came streaking on. Pace lifted his rifle to his shoulder. A shot would be bad, in itself, but not as bad as letting the berserk creature drive headlong into the herd. He gave the horse a few more seconds to veer off. When it failed to do so, he drew a bead and shot. The horse stumbled, then went end over end.

But the damage was done. The silenced din in the foreground gave way to another, lower but equally ominous, behind him. The latter began as a pouring sound, like beans tumbling from a bag, mixed with the bawling of calves and the rumbling of the older cattle. By the time Pace could swing his horse around, the bunch was running, away from the dark monster it still thought to menace it. Hoofs hammered the ground until they beat up the roar of a waterfall. They were carrying the new gather back into the country it had been rounded out of, back among the worked cattle of that afternoon.

Pace saw a rider streak along on the near edge of the herd, trying to gain on the cattle. Swearing steadily, he hazed his horse in the same direction. The stuff was holding on the flanks, letting him bend his efforts toward reaching the point of the run. Someone up there was flailing with his hat and firing his pistol into the air. Pace came up behind him and pitched in. A handful of strong young steers were out front, set on having their own way about it. He saw that the forward rider was Bim, who kept slanting his horse toward the pointers, risking his neck in the effort to turn them. Pace pulled even with him and,

48

together, they began to curve the point away from them slightly.

Men who had been asleep at the camp were catching up. By then the riders already with the cattle had turned them nearly into a flying fishhook. They had already covered a lot of ground, sweeping up worked stuff, leaving dead calves behind. Beyond lay roughs that would spell pure ruin if the steers overran them. The new men threw themselves in on the outside of the crude hook, their lives at stake with each pounding step of the horses. At last they had turned the run into a traveling U. Only a hair-raising distance short of the first roughs, they hammered this on into a revolving but stationary circle.

It was daylight by the time the cattle ran themselves down. But angry, silent men still circled them. Pace and Bim stood by their heaving horses, smoking and not wanting to look at each other. Finally Pace turned and said, "Let's see what we can find out about this."

They mounted and rode back along the slope, frequently finding a dead calf or one so badly hurt they had to put it out of its misery with a bullet. They had ridden quite a distance before they came to the dead horse.

Pace had correctly guessed the form the mischief had taken. The growing light revealed an accompanying insolence that infuriated him. The dried cowhide wore the Bedrock brand. It had once wrapped beef that had gone into hill stomachs. Even worse, he had killed one of his own horses, for it wore the same brand. Someone with incredible brass had lifted it from the *remuda* the wrangler had taken off from camp and left hobbled for the night.

"They brought it onto the slope along that draw," Pace said, pointing. "Where we couldn't see them. Tied that hide to its tail, headed it toward the herd, and whacked it. All the poor critter could think of, after that, was outrunning the thing chasing it. Let's see if we can find out how they worked it."

Pace rode on toward the draw, Bim following reluctantly. They found the place where the horse had been started on its maddened drive toward the herd. There were horse and boot tracks, but nothing else there now. They found a dead cougar on up the draw, directly upwind from where the cattle had been bedded.

"That's what made the steers so jittery all night," Pace remarked bitterly.

The cougar was a shock to Bim. Any good shot could kill one if he managed to tree it. But it had taken a horse to carry this great cat from wherever it had been bagged.

49

Like Pace, Bim knew of but one man in the hills with a
horse that would stand for one on its back. Spud Stevens.

Bim muttered a sick, "Jesus."

They rode back to the herd, which had calmed down
enough to be moved back to the original holding ground.
When this had been done, Pace left four men to handle it,
for the animals were hungry again, thirsty and out of
sorts. The rest of the crew went in to camp, where the
cook had breakfast waiting. They were a silent bunch, and
when a puncher grew tight-lipped he was close to the
exploding point, himself.

CHAPTER 7

Pace aroused curiosity but was asked no questions when, after supper, he saddled a fresh horse and struck off toward Pistol Peak. It was a long way, but he rode without haste, leaving Baldy Slope, then crossing Bear Prairie before he came to the higher country around the peak. He watched his surroundings carefully until the night grew too dark to see. He saw no signs of molestation to the Bedrock cattle strung all along the way.

While this was an unabated worry, it wasn't what had brought him and carried him on into the country above the peak. Having to do over so much hard work that day, hadn't helped his men's tempers a bit. That had told him plainly that the next time something happened, they would be hard to restrain from doing the very thing their slyly hidden enemies wanted.

All that grueling day he had tried to fit the destructive stampede in with Tex Gilgen's burning desire to take over the ranch. The only thing that made sense was that the destruction and disruption were only incidental. Gilgen's original plans had gone quickly and badly awry. He knew he was suspect and, as far as he knew, by Alper, as well. The only prudent move left to him was to start a range war in which he could step in and pick up the pieces. The nesters were already aroused and suspicious. There was plenty of competent help to be had from the outlaws hiding in the badlands. If the Bedrock could be baited into attacking, it would have to take the blame for starting that kind of trouble.

An hour after dark, Pace was in the Sand Creek canyon and hearing the first challenge of the distant hounds. The reminder that no one could come near without somebody in the upcountry knowing it irritated but didn't slow him. They were really cutting loose when he came to the Stevens pocket to see light in the windows of the shack. The door had opened, and a man's figure was framed in the lamplight behind.

Drawing nearer, Pace saw something in the darkness to

51

the right of the door that gave him pause. He had hoped to talk straight to Stevens, to try to help him or, that failing, to warn him for the last time. But they had a visitor. A horse he couldn't identify in the dark, stood there with an empty saddle and trailed reins.

Stevens had expected the oncomer to be anybody but him. When Pace was close enough to be recognized, the man pulled straighter, as if worried about being highlighted in the doorway. He moved a hand over and out of sight behind the doorframe. Pace knew a rifle stood there, leaned against the wall. Then Stevens changed his mind and stepped outside. He shut the door behind him and came down the steps. He yelled at the hounds to shut up. They did, except for nervous whimpering.

"Who's in there you don't want me to see?" Pace asked.

"My company's none of your business," Stevens said in a low voice. "What you doing up here at this time of night?"

"I come to give you a last chance to help yourself." While Stevens had spoken quietly, Pace wanted to be heard in the shack. "Hank Alper would have taken you in the other day, if I'd given the nod. You knew a man had been killed. You knew where they hid the horses. One of your dogs was up there to help 'em. You were open to charges, without that dead cougar on Baldy Slope that only you could have packed there."

Stevens shifted his feet and said scoffingly, "I don't have the faintest notion of what you're talking about."

"The hell you don't," Pace snapped. "So far the sheriff figures like I do. You're being used and can't help yourself. You know this back country like nobody else. They need you, and they know how to make you take orders."

"You're talking foolishness."

"Hardly. Stevens, get yourself and Wendy out of here. I'll buy your setup, and at a good price."

"My place ain't for sale."

"Then take a trip. I'll even pay for it."

Stevens cut a look toward the shack, then said gruffly, "Never mind doing me any favors. I don't need 'em from you."

"Then I'll quit being sorry for you."

"That's all right with me." Stevens straightened his shoulders. "Get out of here, Larabee. This is one nester you won't get rid of easy."

Pace's eyes narrowed. That was confirmation of everything he had surmised. He rode on up the canyon instead of turning back down, resolved to find out who had been

52

in that shack besides Wendy. It was certain that they would watch and suppose that he was going on to Silver Butte.

The grade wasn't steep, and he lifted his horse to a trot. When in a few minutes he came to the bolder nest that had hidden him once before, he turned off the trail, dismounted and led the horse into cover among the rocks. He stood at the head of the horse to make sure it kept quiet when the other one came along. He waited, tense, wary, and wondering if he had had good luck or bad in arriving at the Stevens place just when he did.

Not many minutes had passed, although it seemed a lot of them, when he heard beating hoofs down the canyon. His eyes had long since adjusted to the darkness, but he wasn't set where he could see the approach of the rider. The additional wait crowded his patience, although the rider came swiftly on. He saw in a moment that it was Howie Renner, who must have been at the Stevens shack to set something more in motion. Howie's horse betrayed no awareness of another in the darkened rock patch. Pace waited until Howie had all but vanished on above him, before he mounted and rode out on the trail. He kept the distance. A moment afterward he saw how Howie meant to reach Silver Butte ahead of him.

Howie had vanished into one of the numerous clefts, this one on the right side of the canyon. Pace approached the spot with caution, not trusting that Howie wasn't onto him. When he reached the break he saw that it would barely let a horse and rider squeeze through to the top. He entered it, himself, climbing warily, for Howie might have waited in the slot to make sure he had nobody behind him. But it was empty all the way up.

When he topped out, himself, Pace could see nothing in the limited area that the night let him examine. He pondered whether Howie had headed straight for Silver Butte or had set himself on another course. Pace leaned to the latter possibility. Killing him was still their most burning ambition. The big canyon made a gradual bend from there to where the Silver Butte trail left it. A man riding straight across the bench could be there ahead of anybody sticking to the canyon. Pace struck out in that direction, himself.

He didn't need to see Howie to find his objective. It was safer not to follow close, and his idea was to avoid being where Howie expected him to be when they met. If the man meant to lay for him again, he would be the one caught dead to rights. Pace continued on at a quiet walk, from time to time reining in to see if he could hear the other horse. Nothing came to his ears but the natural, wind-stirred sounds of the uplands. The night was deep enough by then that the moon was coming up. It was getting pretty cold, as well.

He came upon Howie's horse about where he expected it, proving the soundness of his guess. The animal turned its head and whickered, checking Pace's breath, but there had been no avoiding that. If Howie heard it, he would suppose the approaching horse to be down in the canyon. Pace stayed with his own mount only a little farther, then swung down. Taking the rifle from the boot, he left the animal there.

The area was dangerously open. The elevation was too great for sagebrush, and by the canyon, there was none of the timber that skirted the butte. Trusting to Howie's preoccupation with the canyon floor and the man he expected to come off it and climb the draw, Pace crept on. The moon seemed glaringly bright by then. He put himself in Howie's place and judged where he would set himself for a swift, sure shot at a rider in the draw. He moved on toward that point.

He spotted his man with an abruptness that startled him. Howie was faced the other way, his attention riveted on the bottom of the steep, narrow fissure below him. He had murder in his heart, sure enough, and there would be time later to fix up something that would keep him clear of the law. He was openly exposed from above but would be hard to see from below. That was all the advantage Howie asked for. Pace wanted him. If he took him, he would have the concrete evidence he had talked and bluffed about.

His voice stiffened the man even as the words carried forward.

"Howie! Toss that rifle over the bank! Quick about it!"

Howie knew he had no chance to whip around and shoot before he died. What he did was so quick and cunning, Pace didn't have time to grasp it before it was carried out. Instincts born of his wild way of life threw Howie forward, together with the rifle. Pace shot. But even as the sound punched into his ears, Howie disappeared. He had made a headlong dive over the bank into the draw below.

Pace checked the urge to bolt forward. He had ridden up that draw on his other visit to Silver Butte. The talus wasn't steep enough to have given Howie a bad fall. It was too much to expect that the hasty shot had done any damage. Howie had gained cover, and there was none on the open ground on top.

Pace dropped flat, his eyes searching the lip beyond which Howie had dropped. At any moment the man would show himself somewhere, hoping to exploit his regained advantage. Pace had seen nothing when the next shot rent the silence. It was followed by two others in quick succession. Pace frowned. That was a signal of distress recognized everywhere. Howie's resorting to it meant the shots could be heard at the butte.

In deeper trouble than he had anticipated, Pace watched with keening eyes, worried that Howie would only lie doggo until he had drawn help. Then Pace began to work himself backward, still hugging the ground, still expecting his movements to trigger a shot from Howie. When none came, he knew the man had taken a defensive stand below. He was merely watching the lip of the bench in case he was rushed. Pace climbed to his feet. When nothing happened, he moved swiftly to his right.

He crossed the Silver Butte trail in a running crouch. On its far side he cut in again toward the canyon. When he circled back to the draw, he was on the opposite side from where he had been. He reached the lip expecting to see Howie squatting on the far talus. There was no one there, or anywhere in the draw. Howie had played it safe. While waiting for help, he had slipped down into the main canyon. That would keep Pace from escaping that way. If he left the way he had come up, it would let Howie out of his bind.

Pace realized that escape had become his own main problem when he heard, in the far night, the drum of hoofs on the ground. He retraced his course hurriedly to the other side of the trail. He was barely away from it when two riders showed themselves to the west. They were near and coming on fast.

Pace hurried on to his own horse and swung into the saddle. So far they hadn't spotted him, for they continued their drive toward the draw. He rode quietly toward the distant break by which he and Howie had come up from the canyon. He rode reluctantly, for he had raised a dust that he didn't want to let settle until he had gained more from it.

It was highly probable that Gilgen was making Silver Butte his headquarters. If Jinx hadn't been the one with him, others were hanging around there now, too. Much as he detested Jinx, he couldn't quite believe she would take an active part in bloody violence. Her thoughts went in other directions, entirely. When he could no longer see the other riders, he swung away from the canyon and headed for the butte.

He rode almost to the old mine before he stopped, by then screened by timber. There was light in the house. He swung down and left his horse, glad that this family kept no dogs. He left the rifle behind, but his six-gun was in its holster. His first objective was the nearest of the old outbuildings. When he reached it, he stopped again to listen and look about. He seemed to have caused no further disturbance here. He moved up to one of the lighted windows of the house.

He found himself peering into a sitting room. The hour had grown late for hill people, but both women living in the house were there. Stella, Howie's wife, sat by a fire in a rocking chair. She was fat, with blond curls and a baby face. Jinx, who again could have been a boy except for the distinct contradictions, was pacing the floor. Stella looked sleepy and disinterested, but Jinx's excitement was highly evident. She couldn't know what was taking place, but she knew it was some kind of crisis.

There didn't seem to be any more men there, and he went around to the back door. It wasn't locked; few in the West ever were. He opened it gently and stepped into a kitchen. A floorboard creaked as he crossed the room, checking his breath. Apparently the women hadn't heard. He went on and was framed in the doorway to the lighted room before Jinx turned her head and gasped. Her glance dropped to the gun he held in his fist. He didn't feel a bit silly pulling it on them. Jinx, at least, was all trouble.

"Why, Pace!" She smiled at him. "I never had a man come courting me with a gun in his hand!"

She sauntered toward him, but he snapped, "Stop right there. Set still, Stella. It could damned easy slip my mind you're females."

"How you hang onto the idea you could," Jinx murmured. "That's the second time you threatened to. Me, I mean, and I don't care if you shoot Stella. She's so full of booze, it'd be like drilling a whiskey barrel."

"Aw, shut up," Stella said comfortably.

Stella obviously was drunk, and Jinx wasn't feeling as flippant as she was trying to act. Her gaze kept sliding about. He had an idea she would have thrown the lamp at him if it had been in reach.

He said, "Where's your wraps?"

Her eyes widened. "There by the door. Why?"

"Get 'em. You're coming with me." He addressed Stella

56

without taking his eyes off Jinx. "When your men get back, tell 'em I've got this mountain lily. And that I'm tired of dodging their lead."

Jinx's spirit returned. "If you aim to hide behind my skirts, you better let me put some on."

"Shut up and get your wraps."

She sighed, then went over to the rack of hats and coats by the front door. She put on a short coat and a hat with a saucily flipped brim. She knew how to make herself exciting, whatever she wore. The boy's wrappings didn't take a thing away from her allure.

She said, "So long, Stella. See you after the honeymoon. I just can't resist this handsome man and his six-shooter."

CHAPTER 8

Pace made Jinx walk ahead of him, leaving the house the way he had entered it. If she was frightened, she kept it hidden. He took her to the horse corral and made her saddle herself a mount. He made her lead the horse, walking ahead of him, while they moved on out to the timber where he had left his own. He took his rifle from the boot and told her to mount.

"Don't try to make a break," he warned. "All I've got to do is drop your horse. Make me do that, and you're in for a long walk."

"Where we gonna live?" she asked. "The big house on Bedrock?"

While she was swinging up, he lifted the rifle and fired three shots into the air. Her horse shied, and he thought it would bolt, but she held it in. She knew he meant what he had said about shooting it from under her if she tried to get away.

"I'll spot you one thing," she murmured, looking down at him, "you're full of surprises."

He mounted and sent her ahead of him through the trees. She expected to be taken out of the hills, and he wondered what was going through her mind. Well hidden under the pines, he called to her to stop. He rode up abreast of her and dismounted. She looked down at him with a set face.

He said curtly, "Light down."

"Now, look here—!"

"Move."

"You lay a hand on me and—!"

"Down."

She jerked her head, then swung from the saddle, her bravado gone. He told her to trail reins, did likewise, then took her on to where the trees thinned out on the bench. They had been there only a few minutes when they heard hoofs.

"One peep out of you," Pace warned, "and I'll break your neck."

58

In only a moment, three horsemen whipped by, riding pellmell for the butte. As he had hoped, they had mistaken the shots he had fired for a call for help from the house. They passed close enough for him to recognize all three. He had expected Howie and Gilgen. It was the third man who gave him a surprise.

He was Les Baine, a man who hadn't been seen in the country the past two or three years. A self-admitted outlaw, Baine was inordinately vain of his fast gun, which had caused him to leave the country on a sloping horse, the man he had killed having had more friends than he had realized. The furor over that had died down, and Baine seemed to have deemed it safe to return. If he wasn't a principal in the big scheme, he aimed to lend it a hand. That proved that the whole owlhoot, whose hero he was, would pitch in on call. Considering Spud Stevens' distrustful hostility, Gilgen had his fighting forces well lined up.

Looking at Jinx, Pace said, "How long has Baine been back?"

"A while."

"He hanging around the butte because of you? Or for the pickings?"

"Me being there don't pain him." She tried to laugh and shouldn't have. Its forcedness betrayed the fear she was trying hard to hide. "You still want to hang onto me? He's wicked with a six-shooter."

"I've heard about him."

It was only a few moments later when the riders came pounding back from the peak. Stella had told them what had really happened and how neatly they had been fooled. They thought he had used the chance to get away, as Jinx had expected him to do. They would be a long ways down the country before they realized they were on a wild-goose chase.

"You're too foxy for words," Jinx breathed. The vanishing of the men in the far night, the fading away of hoofs, had driven home how completely she had been stripped of the protection she relied on instinctively. "What *are* you after?"

"Looks like I've got it, don't it?"

He took her back through the trees to their horses. Her wariness increased when he shoved his rifle back into its boot. All he did was to pick up the reins of her horse, throw them back on its neck, then give it a whack that sent it galloping off under the trees.

He said, "Get walking."

"You're—turning me loose?" she gasped.

"I wouldn't touch you with a tepee pole coupled onto a wagon tongue."

"Why—why—" She fell silent but remained open-mouthed, her excessive vanity making that impossible to believe and accept. She jerked her head and stepped closer, lifting up her face. "Just you kiss me and say that," she challenged.

"Beat it."

Before he could step away from it, she had her arms around his neck and herself pressed against him. He lifted his hands to shove her away. They moved right on around to the small of her back. He smelled her hair, felt the warmth of her breath, and was all too aware of the several contacts with her slim, firm body. She dropped an arm and brought it up under his shoulder. It gave her grip and balance, and she shot onto her toes, but she merely brushed his mouth with her lips.

She leaned back. "Matter? Something happening to your tepee pole and wagon tongue?"

His hand stabbed down to close on hers, which rested on the gun in his holster. He had practically to crush her wrist before she loosened her fingers. He shoved her back from him. She gave him a look of scornful amusement, turned her back and walked off under the pines.

He stood there, shaking his head and wondering how long it would take him to forget what he had felt.

He had set her afoot, but knew that she would still upset him if she could manage it. He turned to his horse and swung up, shaking his head to clear it. He had something more serious, if less exciting, to think about. There was no estimating when the men would realize their mistake and turn back. Jinx knew that, and if she had got hold of his gun she would have held him there for them.

He stuck to the bench, although he wasn't familiar with it, from there to Pistol Peak. Yet there was a good moon to help him, and there was no need to worry about showing himself openly up there. So he had made good time when he came down into familiar country not far from the peak. He stopped there to rest his horse and roll a cigarette. Thus he heard it, that most frequent of warnings, the drum of hoofs in the distance. It didn't sound like more than one horse, and it was coming fast from east of him.

He rode on to where he could see the trail where it bent and vanished into Cobble Canyon. He had barely concealed himself there among the rocks and brush when the oncoming rider streaked past. His mouth dropped open. It was Wendy Stevens, and she whipped her horse like her

60

life depended on it. Even as he registered this, she disappeared into the canyon. He couldn't conceive of her being so far from home, alone and at that time of night. Nor of her undertaking mischief on the Bedrock summer range, which certainly she had come from.

Then he thought of the three men he had himself sent down this way in driving pursuit of himself. If they hadn't tumbled to the deception, they might have kept up the chase until they decided he had made it to the cow camp. Whatever, there was no point in taking after Wendy. She would scorn his help, even if he could catch her and offer it. But he waited there, intent on seeing for sure what was after her. While he waited, he got shells from a saddle pocket and replaced those he had used at Silver Butte.

He was barely through with this when he had proof that Wendy hadn't merely been in a hurry to get home and to bed. The oncoming horses were traveling just as fast as she had. Pace moved to a position that suited him better. Still sitting his horse and now but thinly covered, he lifted the rifle to his shoulder. They weren't watching anything but the trail they followed. He wondered if, from a distance, they had mistaken Wendy for him. Whatever, he had to let her get back to the Stevens pocket, where she would have her father's help.

He aimed at the leading horse and shot, for it was ridden by Tex Gilgen. It went down in a somersault that sent its rider flying. Pace shot again, not trying to kill a man unless he had to but to rattle and stop them. He had already gained that. Howie and Baine whipped their horses into cover. Another shot sent Gilgen crawling after them. Pace knew they were trying to figure out where he was and waited grimly. He hoped earnestly that they didn't know they had been chasing Wendy. She needed that badly for her future safety. If they had believed it to be himself, they thought that instead of ducking into the canyon, he had turned off and laid for them.

One of them tried a probing shot, and the bullet zipped through the brush to his right. He stifled the urge to shoot back, for there was no sense in helping them locate him. In a moment one of them raised up enough to be seen. Pace had to shoot, and the man dropped fast. They knew he was still there, and more minutes crept by. Then he quietly turned his horse and rode back into the shadows of the peak. They didn't detect this, and if they tried anything more, it would be to follow him.

Leaving the peak, he cut wide of where he had left them. He was a mile east of there before he lifted the speed of his horse, heading straight for the cow camp. He didn't slow to a walk until he was almost there, where he had to be quieter because of the herd. The campfire burned low, but there was the figure of a man sitting there by it. He rode on to the night band, unsaddled his horse, rubbed it down with the blanket, and put it on picket.

When he looked up Bim stood there. Pace felt a momentary gratification. The boy had been worried about him and hadn't gone to bed.

"Man," Bim said hotly, "I wish you weren't so goddam lonehanded. Where you been?"

Pace told him about it, staying where they were so they wouldn't disturb the sleepers. He omitted only that moment when he had held Jinx Renner in his arms, as excited and nearly as witless as any man would have been.

"You were wrong about her," he concluded. "And I was wrong about Wendy Stevens. That girl's all there."

Bim looked at him keenly. "How you figure?"

"She helped me out of that trap in the Sand Creek canyon. I think tonight she was trying to get word to you or somebody that I'd gone up to Silver Butte with Howie on my heels. You said she despises you now. But there's somebody she cares about down here, and it sure as hell isn't me."

Bim shook his head. "Spud wouldn't have let her."

"Then she sneaked off and run into those three and had to turn back."

Bim scratched his jaw. "If they know that, she's in trouble."

"She sure is. Maybe I threw them off, maybe I didn't. I wish that muleheaded hermit would at least send *her* out of the country."

"She wouldn't go. You've always been blind to them and some of the rest. They're as inclined to hang and rattle as you are."

They went in to the fire. Bim, at last, was ready for bed and turned in. Pace poured himself a cup of coffee and sat down with it and a cigarette. Only then did he notice that his knee didn't hurt him like a thing on fire, the way it usually did when he was worn out. He wondered if Jinx had been right when she said he held onto it to nurse his grudge against the hill people.

To accept that he would have to admit that it was a grudge. He couldn't believe it. He had moved cattle into the Bedrock when there had been nothing but outlaws up there, and he had held his own against them. Only when the owlhoot became less active and the rest of the country more settled, had the nesters dared to filter in to squat on isolated spots he still had a right to call his. He had already shown them forbearance, which they had repaid with suspicion, hostility and mischief culminating in the damaged knee and now a threat to his very survival. Theirs was the grudge, the universal resentment of the weak and incompetent for the strong and capable.

CHAPTER 9

It was, from outward appearances, as smooth and efficient a roundup as Pace had ever run in the Bedrock. He watched the work at the branding fires with the satisfaction of knowing that the calf crop was one of his best. This he knew to be no smile bestowed on him by fortune. It resulted from his own careful planning and control.

The gather had moved off Baldy Slope and was halfway across Bear Prairie. There had been no molesting since the run on Baldy at the start of the branding. He would like to think that this was because the schemers in the hills had got as good as they had sent. Stubborn sense told him that, more likely, they were only waiting. The time wasn't far ahead when this job would be finished. Then most of his men would return to the lower basin to start haying and doing all the other work of summer.

Froggy Jorgensen, who had been roping, walked over. He was pulling on a newly made cigarette, and dust had made his sweating face into a wrinkled, runneled mask. Taking the weed from his lips, he said, "Some different to the first herd we brung up here to summer."

Pace glanced at him in appreciation. With the death of Durnbo, Jorgensen was one of the few left who could be called charter members of the outfit.

"Yeah," he agreed with a grin. "We were sure a gunnysack outfit, that year."

Jorgensen lapsed into silence, a button-lip always. Pace turned and walked to his waiting horse. For the first time, he sensed something that Bim felt for the hired men. Drifters came and went, interested mainly in financing their own rootless lives. Hands like Jorgensen, Durnbo, Swede O'Brien and a few others adopted a ranch, if they liked it, and stayed with it down the years. They took pride in it, felt a concern for it, and for no greater personal return than their wages.

He wondered what worked in him to shut them out. Why he kept them in their places and always aware that they were minor cogs in a concern he owned and ran. It was the same thing that, along the way, had shut out Bim. Whatever it was, it was more indispensable now than ever. He had seen signs in plenty that none of them had forgotten the killing of Durnbo. Or the stampede and the wearing need to guard constantly against further mischief. The work, itself, was tough enough.

Riding east from the branding camp, he reflected that this foment in the men was what Tex Gilgen wanted. It was what he had relied on, what he would keep working on until he had exploded the outfit into an attack on the hill country. Gilgen's tactics were those of the gunman, Les Baine: to provoke attack in hope of meeting it with overwhelming skill and force. The problem was to meet further aggravations, by some hook or crook, and deny the man the bloody range war he wanted.

The throwbacks on Baldy Slope had settled in the several localities that the various bunches had adopted for the summer. Pace found no signs of new trouble, but when he neared Kettle Wells, one of the slope's waterings, he grew puzzled. The wells lay under a rim and were once flowing springs that, long since, had dwindled to water holes kept level and sweet by the weakened vein. Even as he approached from the open ground, he saw the stick that had been pounded into the ground there, with a piece of paper tacked to it.

He rode up with narrowed eyes to tense instantly. The sign showed a crude skull and crossbones. The word POISON had been lettered under this by an unskilled hand.

His first reaction was a searching look about. The wells served a large section of the slope. While there was no stock near at the moment, the watering was visited often and regularly. There were no carcasses in evidence. He pondered this a moment, then realized that the water hadn't yet been poisoned. This was a more cunning and effective blow. It was a warning of what could happen, not only here but at any or all of the waterings on which his summer grazing depended.

He rode back to camp with a darkened face and lowered spirit. The sly taunt of the warning was as infuriating as the Bedrock horse they had used to stampede his cattle. It reminded him, also, of the mocking disdain Jinx Renner had used on him the night he forced her to accompany him into the timber.

Suppertime was at hand when he reached the camp, with the tired men not on herd gathered at the wagon. He spotted Bim among them, signed to him and rode on to the *remuda*. Bim came up while he was still unsaddling. It

65

came to Pace that their only communication, of late, was when there was trouble. He told Bim what he had seen at Kettle Wells.

"How can you be sure the water hasn't already been poisoned?" Bim asked, deeply worried.

"Well, I didn't feel inclined to take a drink of it," Pace admitted. "But a cow can't read. If they'd really poisoned the potholes, there'd be plenty of dead stuff around there by now. They were only reminding us what they can do any time they want. Spud Stevens keeps strychnine on hand for his wolfing. And we can't guard every watering we've got and run a calf roundup."

Bim said with a grimace, "It always comes back to Spud."

Pace nodded. "He's their live bait, the one they want us to pitch into. Then they can all line up on his side. Why he puts up with it I don't know, but there's got to be a good reason."

"Sure." Bim's voice was brittle with anger. "Spud figures he's picking the lesser of two evils. What do we do? Quit branding and start guarding the water?"

"We hire more men."

Bim gave him a sour eye. "It's late in the season to pick up good ones."

"A man don't need to be a cowhand to stand guard. Just tough enough. There's plenty of that breed around Rowel."

They went to the fire. The men looked at them curiously, knowing from the private talk that something new was up. Bim's set face confirmed their suspicions. But nobody asked questions. Pace ate his meal, brooding on the new problem. Most of the waterings were spring fed. The springs, themselves, flowing constantly, couldn't be poisoned for long. But the ponds he had built to store their output, and from which the stock drank, were another matter. They all had to be protected, now that notice had been given. He would have to find a dozen new men to mount clock-around guards. He could stand the expense, but it was a drain, and an even heavier drain on time and energy. That, another turn of the screw, was what his enemies wanted.

After supper he saddled a fresh horse and struck out for Rowel. The evening was warm, with evidence of the transition from spring to summer everywhere in sight. Haying would be underway in another month. He might have to hire hayers, for the first time, and keep his regular crew on the summer range. A lot of other things he would have to let go for that year. The impatience his men felt began to rake him.

He was still close to headquarters when he saw, ahead

66

and coming toward him, two riders whom he quickly recognized as Spud and Wendy Stevens. Their being on that trail at that hour was of no special significance. It was the route most of the hill people took to and from Dalles City or, now, Rowel. He saw them react to him by alerting and staring forward. But they kept riding on. Hostility built in him as he rode on toward them. Yet it was tempered by his concern for Wendy and his gratitude for her help that day in the canyon.

They would have ridden stonily by, but when Pace stopped and signed them, they reined in. Wendy wore a split skirt and looked prettier and more feminine than in the hill garb he was so used to seeing her in. She kept her eyes lowered, but he hoped this was from natural feminine shyness rather than a dislike of acknowledging his existence. Spud was openly glowering.

Pace had intended to ask him if he had been sent to town to build up his stock of strychnine. Instead, he felt himself prompted to try again to make the man quit the country so Wendy wouldn't be bound by loyalty to stay there with him. Suddenly this seemed as important as the cattle and the survival of the ranch, itself.

He said quietly, "When are you going to wake up, Spud, to what you're doing to your daughter?"

Wendy looked up quickly, somewhat startled by his statement. But Pace didn't intend to betray the favors she had done, if not for him then for Bim through him. He looked at her with a gentleness that conveyed his thanks. She flushed and lowered her eyes. He had a feeling she knew who it was who broke up the pursuit of her, that night at the Cobble Creek gap.

Her father's face had grown more set. "When," he retorted, "will you learn to tend to your own affairs? Seems to me there's enough of them to keep a man busy."

"You're a queer one, Spud," Pace said. "Too proud to run but not too proud to be used by the scum at Silver Butte."

Wendy lifted scornful eyes. "Why not? We're scum, too."

"No, you're not."

"What changed your mind about that?"

"You."

"I'm what I always was," she said tartly. "And what my father is and most of my neighbors are. So get back on your high horse and forget Wendy Stevens. A while ago you were scared to death she'd contaminate your family."

Spud flung her a look of appreciation. She started her horse, and he followed her.

Pace rode on, his mind puzzled and his feelings scrambled. When it came to himself, there was as much hostility in Wendy as there was in her father. He was no longer certain that they were only helplessly caught in the war against the ranch. Wendy had balked at seeing him murdered in treachery. The destruction of the ranch was something else, a drive that might have been strengthened by Bim's jilting her for Jinx Renner.

It had grown dark when he rode onto the crowded, noisy streets of Rowel. After the serenity of the country night, the raw town was offensively out of keeping. Passing along the main thoroughfare, he eyed the floating riffraff that populated the place on a weekend night. From these, the men he was being forced to hire would have to come.

Lacking time to do his own seeking and sifting, he rode directly to Joe Dollar's saloon. A transplant from Dalles City, Dollar's establishment had long been a clearing house for local communication. Word left there of what he wanted would get results. He took care of this and was on the point of starting for home when he changed his mind.

There were lighted windows over the Fandango, across and down the street from where he had tied his horse. This meant that Arliss was in her private quarters, rather than the saloon downstairs. Word would soon be around that the Bedrock was hiring guns, and she would hear of it quickly. He had felt alienated from her ever since she confessed to being the estranged wife of Tex Gilgen. But he owed it to her to explain why he was taking on extra men.

He was nearly to her outside stairs when the door of the saloon itself swung open and two men came out. They turned in the other direction, but for a moment Pace stood stockstill on the walk. They were Gilgen and the returned gunman, Les Baine. Gilgen, he noticed, walked with a limp. Pace hoped this was a result of the spill he gave the man when he shot the horse from under him. He hoped the limp would be as permanent as the one Gilgen, or someone else, had given him. The two men were talking animatedly. Pace turned toward the stairs with a scowl. A part of his annoyance came from Gilgen's use of Arliss's place as a hangout when he was in town.

Pace climbed the stairs with his anger turning toward Arliss for putting up with it. She had plenty of spirit. Gilgen's coveting of the money she had made in Colorado would naturally concern her. But it would hardly cow her into a meek acceptance of his whims. From what she had divulged, they sometimes met and talked privately. Pace

68

found it hard to dislodge the suspicion that she still had some feeling for the man. It angered him to think of what she had refused to be to him and had been to Gilgen and might, in her heart, still long to be to the man.

Pace nearly turned back down the stairs, feeling himself to be in no mood to see and talk with her. Then he saw the cowardice of this and went on to the door at the landing above him. Arliss took a moment about answering his rap. Then she stood there, looking at him with an expression he had never seen on her face before.

Then she turned half away from him and said in confusion, "Pace, would you mind? I'm not feeling well and—" She lowered her eyes.

But he had already seen it, the bruise over the bone of her cheek. He pushed on inside.

CHAPTER 10

Arliss walked slowly across the room and seemed reluctant to turn again and face him. Pace shut the door, went over and, his hands roughly on her shoulders, swung her around. She looked up with a forced smile.

"Correction," she said, with an attempt at lightness. "I mean I'm not looking so good. The silliest thing happened. I bumped against a cupboard door."

"Who hit you?" Pace thundered. "Your husband?"

"Don't be preposterous. I just got careless."

"Then why did you try to hide it from me?"

She tossed her head. "I'm a woman and I look awful, that's why."

He dropped his hands. She went over and sat down. His blood thundered in his chest and ears, for he knew she was lying. He stood glowering over her for that, for being Gilgen's wife, for having a part of herself she kept from him. He wanted to find Gilgen and tear him apart.

"What are you doing in town in midweek?" she asked.

He walked over to a window, trying to get hold of himself. Then he told her, for that was what he had come to see her about. She listened, quiet and somber. "Now," he added, looking at the livid bruise, "I want to know why he hit you. Then I'm going to make him wish he'd never come to these parts."

"Pace, now!" She looked stricken. "Really, it *was* the silly thing I said. I just bumped—"

"Horse sweat! Did he demand his family rights?"

She colored and dropped her eyes. He towered over her again. She looked up miserably.

"You're being ridiculous. If your jealousy wasn't so dangerous, I'd be flattered. Tex hasn't touched me since I left him, not even with his fist. You've got to believe that. If you braced him over me, think of the scandal, if nothing else. Believe me. For my sake?"

"Want to know what I believe?" he said heavily. "You may have felt you had to leave him, but you never forgot him as a man."

"Oh, you males." She sprang up, her eyes searching his and a faint smile on her lips. "Get hold of yourself, or you're going to do something dreadful. I've already brought enough down on our heads. You needn't be jealous of any man in any way. Can't you believe *that?*"

"Hardly."

"I'm ready to prove it, Pace." She drew in a tremulous breath. "Well? Haven't you wanted to kiss me?"

"A thousand times."

"That's a tall order. You better get started on it."

She moved closer, lifting her mouth, her arms. Something swept through him like wildfire. His arms clamped about her, and his wits quit him. There was no quick brushing of the lips from her, as there had been from Jinx when she tried to get hold of his gun. Arliss came completely against him, each touching point a heady excitement. Her moist lips waited, received, then returned his searching kiss warmly. Her body was unresisting when he drew her yet closer. He could feel the beating of a heart under the soft mound against his chest.

Yet his flitting memory of Jinx had an effect. Arliss, too, wanted to disarm him, for she was deathly afraid of his bracing Gilgen. Maybe she knew Baine of the notoriously fast gun was in town with Gilgen that evening. Maybe she didn't want the secrets of the past revealed, as they might be if a man were killed because of her. Or maybe she really cared but had repressed and concealed it because she was, in legal fact, a married woman.

Whatever, her lips told him a little but no more than her tongue ever had. He lifted his head and stared down at the bruise on her lifted face. It told him exactly what it had before.

He said gruffly, "Thanks. I'll look forward to the other nine hundred and ninety-nine."

"You don't have to leave yet," she murmured.

"It's a long ride to the summer range, and branding starts at daylight."

Worry showed in her eyes again. "You're hanging onto your foolish notion."

"I don't call it foolish. Gilgen roughed you up tonight over something between the two of you. I seen him leave here with Les Baine. If I hadn't chanced along, I'd never have known about this thing on your cheek. You don't have to put up with that or even with his coming to your place. Either you've still got feeling or you're scared of him."

"Yes, I'm scared of him." She turned and walked away,

71

her shoulders slumped. She swung and looked at him with tear-bright eyes. "And I'm nearly as scared of you."

"Me? Why?"

"He could divorce me for leaving his bed and board, and all that, but he'll never do it. I have no grounds for divorcing him that would hold up in court. He was cruel to me, but I never let anybody else know that. He was unfaithful, but I never had any real proof."

"Then I'll make a widow of you."

"That's just it!" she cried. "You cling to that mood, no matter what I do or say! Pace, don't you see? It wouldn't free me. If you killed a man to get me, I could no more marry you than I can now. And if he killed you, I'd die." She came to him again, lifting stirring eyes. "I can be your wife in everything but name. I'm ready to be. Now."

He looked at her dazedly. "You're really cornered."

"I will be if you make me the bone of contention between you and Tex Gilgen. I know you can keep him from destroying the Bedrock. Afterward I want us to be more than partners. The past weeks have shown me that."

She lifted her arms around his neck. He held her again, but it wasn't the same, nor was the kiss she gave him. Something of grim significance lay beneath her ardor and offer. A week ago, a day ago, he would have sworn that he would take her under any circumstances. But he didn't want her with this disturbing cloud of mystery surrounding them.

"Now?" she whispered.

He said evasively, "We better take a dally on this till after the dust settles."

She stepped away with slumping shoulders. "Then will you promise not to raise more dust than you need to, to protect our ranch?"

"I can't promise a thing, but I'll tell you this. I aim to get my horse and head for the back country when I leave here."

She sighed. "That's the best I can get from you, I guess."

He left quickly, not looking at her again in fear of forgetting everything else and staying. Using the outside stairs again, he went down to the benighted street. He hardly saw the street, although it displayed the same assortment of rough characters in a raw, new town. His arms still tingled from the feel of her. Yet he couldn't forget that this was the way they had felt after he held Jinx Renner that night in the hills. The two weren't alike by any stretch of the imagination. Yet each possessed an unfathomable quality that warned of calculation.

72

He passed along crowded hitching rails until he came to the one where he had left his horse. He was loosening the tie when he recognized the lounging, gangling figure beyond the moving contingent on the walk. Les Baine stood there with his back tipped against a building wall. He had his hat pushed forward on his head and was drawing on the short end of a cigar. He was watching with narrowed eyes, his expression mute and unchanging. The man had seen the Bedrock brand on the horse and had waited for its rider.

Then Baine came across the sidewalk.

"Howdy, Larabee," he said in a tone wholly amiable. "What's this I heard at Joe Dollar's about you hiring more men?"

"What's your interest, Baine?" Pace snapped.

"Curiosity, maybe," Baine said lazily. "Or maybe I figured we could have a little talk."

"Not us." Pace ducked under the tie bar to mount.

"Wait." Baine pressed closer to the wooden rail. "Why don't you just give me a contract to protect your water and handle the details?"

Pace turned back to him. There was a sly smile on the man's slashed mouth. He was offering the hire of his gun to the highest bidder.

"What's the matter, Baine?" Pace asked. "Fall out with Tex Gilgen? I saw you two together this evening."

Baine shrugged. "Gilgen's nothing to me, one way or the other. He only hopes to have wherewithal. You already got it."

"I see. And if I tell you to go to hell?"

"I'll help *him* get it."

"Then I reckon you're going to help him get it."

"Didn't think you were that stupid, Larabee." Baine shook his head. "What I hear, you've made monkeys out of that bunch so far."

"You were in the pack that chased me the other night."

The gunman grinned. "Call that a chase? Seems to me we were only out exercising our saddles. How about it, Larabee? They think the owlhoot's behind them. But it ain't if I tell it it ain't. I can give you protection as long as you need it."

"At a fancy price."

"It's a valuable ranch. Worth buying insurance for."

Pace stared at him. True to his trade, Baine would betray his present confederates if the price was right and do it cheerfully. He would be loyal unto death to his new allegiance as long as the profits were in sight. It was tempting. Rob Gilgen and Renner of the backing of the outlaw country, and the nesters would weasel out fast.

"Where's Gilgen now?" Pace asked.

"Dunno. He was in a mean temper. I liked my own company better."

Pace's eyes narrowed. "Mean temper over what?"

"You got me, Larabee. He's got a lot of things spewing in him he don't talk about. All I want to know is do I buy chips in his game or yours?"

He rode to the end of the street wondering why he had so quickly turned the man down. For one thing, Baine could hire out his gun to both sides at once, working strictly in his own interests. Or the offer could have been a clever move engineered by Gilgen, intended to lead his victim into believing he had bought protection that wouldn't be there. But that wasn't all of it. It just wasn't in him to save himself that way. It wasn't how the Bedrock had got started, and it wasn't how it would survive.

Presently the countryside had wrapped him in its welcome solitude. He rode swiftly, yet at a gait his horse could keep up. The stars had emerged in a vast spread of pinpoints of light. On all the horizons were landmarks known to him so well. The comfort of the long familiar began to loosen his tensions. He pulled a cigar from his shirt pocket and got it ignited.

He began to think of Bim. Now that he had known a couple of women in a way he never had before, he could better understand the heady forces at work in the boy. His own wits surely hadn't stood firm and steady when he had been all arms and body and searching lips. It struck him that there were other parallels between himself and the brother he had lost. A while ago he had brushed aside an offer of protection. The desire to fight his own battles was in Bim, too. In his case the protection hadn't been offered, it had been forced on him. Protection from the mistakes he might make, his own and in what was important to the ranch.

It was well past midnight when ranch headquarters rose before him. He decided to stop there and catch some sleep before riding on into the hills. The scatter of buildings looked lonely with the crew off on roundup. But old Calhoun, who had been left behind to keep an eye on things, would be asleep in the bunkhouse. Pace rode in quietly, put his horse in the corral, and walked across the compound to the big house.

The huge main room smelled stuffy and shut up. He went through without striking a light and climbed the stairs to

74

the balcony and his room. He lit a lamp there, yawning and turned sleepy. It seemed ages since he had known the comforts of home life, such as he had known them here. He hung his gun rig and dropped his hat on one chair, then sat down on another chair to draw off his boots. He lifted his head and stared.

Something lay on the pillow on the bed, a piece of paper. Frowning, he rose and went over. A hand showing no great amount of education had left a note there. He read it.

"You got a real soft bed. Almost sorry I talked you out of making off with me."

He straightened, his eyes bugged. It couldn't be. It was too preposterously daring even for Jinx Renner. But who else would know he had abducted her and made her think for a while that he was taking her with him? It had to be Jinx. She had been here and slept in his bed. Leaving her haunts behind to bedevil him. Ascertaining which was his room by the size of the clothes hanging in his wardrobe.

He turned in, the haunts shut stubbornly from his mind. When he awakened at daylight he got out of bed hastily, as though he had awakened in a graveyard. He dressed, clumped downstairs and went over to the cookhouse. Old Calhoun was there, making breakfast.

"Seen your horse in the corral," Cal said. "How's branding going?"

"No hitches." Pace stared at the oldster. He was no faithful retainer, kept on out of gratitude through his declining years. He had simply wandered in one day, riding the grub line, and Pace had told him to stick around. "Did you let Jinx Renner spend a night here?"

Calhoun grinned sheepishly. "Well, come to think of it, I did. She ride in the other night saying she'd been to Rowel and was too tuckered to make it home. Why? Something missing?"

"She—left a note."

Pace emptied the plate the old man put down in front of him and drained the coffee cup. He could picture a bundle of energy like Jinx being too tired to make it to Silver Butte. He saddled his horse, which had fed and watered in the corral, and struck out for the summer range.

The riders had gone out on circle when he reached the roundup camp. The calves gathered the afternoon before were going under the hot iron. Bim wasn't around, but Pace didn't ask about him. The boy was going to be allowed more head from there on.

Swede O'Brien was tallying. When he saw Pace he left the fire and came over.

75

"Bim said to tell you," he reported, "that they're cleaning out Near's Coulee, this forenoon."

Pace nodded. A ramrod hadn't ought to have to report his every move. Yet Bim always felt he had to do so. Like a ranch kid forbidden to go anywhere or do anything without asking permission first or making a full account afterward. Pace wondered why he hadn't noticed when Bim stopped being a kid. He decided against riding up to the coulee to see how it was going, which was his inclination. From there on Bim could run the roundup. If they missed a few calves, it wasn't as important as the damage he had been doing to the boy.

He said, "All right. If I'm not back by noon, tell him I decided to ride a few waterings."

CHAPTER 11

Bear Prairie had been cleaned up and the roundup, that morning, was starting at Pistol Peak, the roughest of the foothill ranges. It was badly broken country and difficult to ride, let alone to sweep for cattle. And it lay directly against the nester country and the owlhoot on above.

Moreover, in spite of his efforts to avoid it, Pace had been forced to strip his roundup crew in order to post guards in pairs at each of his half-dozen main waterings. Joe Dollar had used a fair judgment in the men he sent out. But before he hired a one of them, Pace had made his own appraisals, and some of them he had sent back to town. Of those he hired, he soon sent two more packing because something about them bothered him. He wanted no firebrands nor did he want his enemies to plant an agent or so on him. He had wound up with only eight new men whom he felt he could trust.

No attempt had been made to molest the water, so far, but none needed to be made. The vexatious necessity the danger imposed was like a mustard plaster applied to flesh and nerves already raw and sore, not only to him but to the men. Under the grueling, windup work at Pistol Peak the men were apt, at any moment, to take the bit in their own teeth. And that was exactly what Tex Gilgen wanted to happen.

From the saddle of the horse he had just taken off picket, Pace watched the last pair of riders fade in the morning distance. He had kept his promise to himself and was leaving the roundup work to Bim. He confined himself to trouble shooting, keeping tabs on the range already worked, and the water holes everywhere. That didn't mean that he could keep from watching the roundup closely, sometimes critically. Compulsively, he did a little prowling and secret checking, guilty though it made him feel.

He left the camp that morning to ride toward the Cobble Creek gap. He hadn't forgotten the stash-hole where he and the sheriff had found his horses. He had seen no sign of rustling, nor had the men reported any, since then. He had decided that the schemers in the hills had postponed that activity until there were fewer Bedrock men racking around. But he wanted to take an unadvertised look at the hideout that morning.

None of the men were working near the gap. So, once he was out of sight of the camp, Pace rode openly toward it. The sky over the break in the distant rim was the deepest of blues. Already the rocky country falling toward the John Day was simmering in summer heat. But at that hour up there, the air was pleasant and laden with the exotic scents of the high desert.

Before he entered the gap, he stopped for a moment by the badly carrioned remains of the horse he had shot from under Tex Gilgen. Somebody had taken away the saddle, bridle and blanket. He went on into the gap and its shadows, riding without hurry. This time nobody expected him, and that was a help. But he hadn't forgotten the noisy dogs in the Stevens pocket.

He rode quietly until he neared the creek forks. There he reined in and listened carefully. There was no evidence of his having been picked up by the distant dogs. He continued on, keeping to Cobble Creek and feeling himself tighten up. He passed the point where the water slid along against narrow rock walls and splashed steadily ahead. When he came to the hidden spit and flat where he had climbed a fissure to the bench above, he paused again.

Still in the water, he studied the sand and rock. There were no tracks or droppings other than relics from the stay his horses had made on the bench above. This relieved his slight concern about having been whittled on without having noticed anything wrong. He moved out of the creek and started his horse up the notch.

He was about to top out, with nothing having warned him, when he had the stomach-shriveling feeling of reliving history. Somewhere above him, and not nearly as far away as the Stevens pocket, hounds cut loose in their peculiar, nerve-grating chorus. Not one, as it had been the other time, but angry canine voices in numbers. It even scared his horse, which stopped and shied backward. Pace didn't urge it on. His first thought was that Spud had chanced to be over here with his pack, after some varmint. A more chilling thought was that they were still using the hideout, still relying on sentry dogs to warn of intruders.

He had to know what it was.

Turning his horse in the narrow notch, he picked his way back down to the creek. He was worried, but that was nothing to his mounting anger. If he had been losing stuff, in his assumption that they were laying off that until after roundup, he would kick himself from here to yonder. He lacked Hank Alper's help this time, but he hesitated only a moment before riding on up the canyon seeking another way to climb out. If there was one, it would be at some distance, for Alper had been unable to find one nearby that other time.

It proved to be a considerable distance, and the sound of dogs had faded out, before he came to another natural exit. This was in a stretch where the canyon widened slightly because of slides of rotten rock. He found a point where he and the horse could get up if he led the animal, although it would be a treacherous place if he had to beat a fast retreat again. He dismounted and tackled it, having to prospect slowly up along the high talus. When he came on top he was badly dislocated, for the empty scene around him was unfamiliar country.

He waited until he and the horse had got back their wind, then remounted. By then he had made a rough guess that he was farther south than he had been that day with the sheriff. The quickest way to get his bearings was to ride west until he found the Sand Creek trench with which he had grown familiar. That would put him dangerously close to Silver Butte, where he had already used as much luck as he could expect. But he had to determine what was happening on the north tip of the bench, and why it was still being guarded so carefully.

He rode with the sun on his left shoulder until he came to what he judged to be the old trail to the upper John Day mining camp which Hank Alper had described. Reassured as to where he was, he headed along the length that would take him to the Sand Creek canyon. In only a few moments the surroundings began to stir memories. Not far ahead was where he had come up from Sand Creek with Alper. He turned northward.

When he raised the belt of trees screening the north tip, he reined in, unable to ride closer without arousing the pestiferous hounds. Casting about, he picked out the tallest rock crop near him, rode to it and left his horse on its blind side. He climbed the rocks, working his way to the top. It was to find, as he had hoped, that the landfall let him see beyond the concealing trees.

In the stretch made visible, he saw nothing that hadn't been there when he and Alper left it with the horses. If there were cattle there now, some would be in sight. If stuff was being picked off Pistol Peak and rushed on out, there would be no point in guarding the place so carefully. There was something else there that had to be kept secret. If not in the open area cut from view, it was in among the trees. There wasn't a chance of determining what it was unless he went in shooting and lived long enough to look about. His worried impatience nearly goaded him into that.

It came to him that he had a problem in getting back to Pistol Peak from where he was. Whether he used Cobble or Sand Creek, he would arouse the hounds again and, this time, whoever was with them would be more alert. He would have to cross Sand Creek and go down the far bench, the way he had escaped from Silver Butte on his most recent visit. He rode south again, toying with the idea of bringing a picked group of men up there that night, for a surprise raid on the bench tip. If he couldn't destroy whatever was being prepared, he could at least find out what it was.

He crossed Sand Creek Canyon at one of the several places where he had learned it could be done, working always downcountry. When he came up on the Silver Butte side, he began to pick at an idea. While he had descended somewhat toward the basin, the terrain on this side of the canyon was higher than that which he had left.

He scanned the timber skirting the butte and running well below it, then picked out the tallest tree in sight. Cutting into the obscurity of the timber, he rode toward this sentinel. When he reached it he found, as he had feared, that it crowned too high for him to scale it. Unless—he eyed the stump of a broken limb far above his head. Loosening his catch rope from the saddle, he looped it and began casting. Half a dozen times the rope fell limply about him. Then the loop caught.

He took the field glasses off the saddle, hung the strap over his shoulder, and went up the rope hand over hand. Perched on the rotten, broken limb, he drew up the rope and began again, managing in a moment to get the rope across one of the nearest living branches above him. It still seemed a slim prospect, but his curiosity and natural stubbornness kept him at it. By sending ripples up the rope, he managed to work the upper end down within reach. A moment afterward he had climbed on up. Balanced against the rough bark of the trunk, he rested and caught his breath. Then he wove on up through the thick limbs until he reached the highest one he could trust with his weight. He took the glasses from the case and set them to his eyes.

A grim smile flitted on his mouth, but he wasn't much surprised. He was, as he had judged, almost abreast the

80

Stevens pocket. At his height it seemed hardly more than a shallow hole scuffed out of the rugged terrain. The shack and other structures were toys. He regarded this but briefly, then settled his attention on the land beyond. It climbed through rocks and scraggly brush and trees to the bench. The belt of trees was slightly to his right, and he could see the entire sweep cut off from him before.

He fiddled with the glasses, trying to bring the far scene nearer. It appeared to be a large camp at the edge of the timber. He studied it closely, making out a pole corral—a generous shelter made from tarps stretched on poles—and what appeared to be a pile of provisions. There were no horses in the corral or out grazing. There were only two men in evidence, although there might be others lolling about. Apparently they had taken the short outburst of the hounds to have been caused by some animal, for there was no look of excitement.

Pace kept his glasses on the scene for long moments without adding to his understanding. This didn't stem his suspicions. The thing had the look of a base camp designed for some degree of permanence. That seemed queer when Silver Butte was only a mile or two distant. Then it came to him with an impact that made his jaw drop open. By touching off the hounds, he had himself emptied the camp of everyone with reason not to want to be seen, especially by the sheriff. They would be men from the backhills whom Howie Renner wouldn't care to have caught frequenting Silver Butte. Men with such twitchy consciences wouldn't come this close to civilization without a good place to hide themselves and with every possible safeguard.

This was Gilgen's main fighting force, around which he planned to organize the nesters, moved down to the very edge of Bedrock Ranch. It was easy to guess the identity of its immediate commander. Pace had only to recall the look in Les Baine's eyes that night on the street in Rowel. He wondered if they were going to attack without waiting for the aggravated assault by the ranch that they had failed to bring off.

His mind protesting the conclusions it had to draw, Pace worked his way down to the ground and his horse. They were conclusions his men would draw the minute they learned of this. The crew couldn't be expected to work Pistol Peak, or in any other part of the basin, under the guns of such a hostile, unscrupled force. Nor could he wait passively, himself. A man in his right mind would attack before they knew he was onto them and destroy the camp and at least scatter the recruited gunfighters.

81

"What in tarnation were you doing up there?" a voice asked. It was female. "Do you collect eagle eggs?"

Pace whirled, his shoulders rising, his fingers spreading above his gun. But Jinx Renner held, instead of a gun, a bouquet of wild flowers in her hands. She had been on the far side of the tree and stepped around quietly. If his horse had reacted, he hadn't noticed it in his absorption. She was smiling prettily above the flowers she held against a chest he tried to keep his eyes away from.

"How did you know I was here?" he blurted.

She dimpled. "I reckon my heart told me."

"Cut it out, Jinx." His breathing had started up again. If she had been armed, he would be in trouble. As it was, he could handle her. "You were just out picking flowers in the woods, I reckon."

She nodded. "That's what I was out doing, but I seen you come up from the canyon. I figured you'd come back to steal me, after all, and I better make myself handy."

"My bed isn't that soft."

Her smile brightened. "You been home and found my note. Were you up in that tree trying to get a look at me? I like to take my bath in the crick. I sort of think the word's around."

"Oh, for God's sake."

"You're blushing."

"You're cute. And an eyeful. So supposing you stop trying to convince me of that. Just tell me what's going on on the bench, over there past Spud Stevens'."

"Is that all you climbed that tree for? Well, Les Baine's setting up a homestead over there. Says he's sick and tired of a footloose life. Something takes even you tough ones in time, Pace. You should make a note of that."

"I'll make my own notes and, if you don't mind, I'm in a hurry."

"But I do mind." A hand dropped from behind the flowers. It held a small and ugly gun. "You set me afoot once. I'm debating if I should return the favor or take you home with me for a pet."

Pace blew out his cheeks. A girl as pretty and provocative as she wouldn't be out alone in the woods, in a country like this, without a means of protecting herself. She had taken him in neatly, and she must know that if she turned him over to her confederates he was as good as dead.

He didn't hesitate. He turned his back deliberately and stepped to his horse. In the saddle, he looked down at her coolly.

"Why didn't you shoot, Jinx?" he asked.

The look on her face was too tangled for him to take apart. He rode away from her, leaving the timber and heading on downcountry, aware at last of how hard his blood crashed in his ears.

CHAPTER 12

Pace couldn't sleep, or maybe it was a case where he didn't want to sleep. Every time he drifted off, Jinx Renner materialized. In dream form she was even more tauntingly alluring than in life, leading him on, bringing him up short, laughing at the feelings that made an idiot of him. Twice since he turned in, the only escape from her had been to wake up.

He sat up in the blankets and fumbled for the makings of a cigarette. His men lay around him, drugged by fatigue, untroubled by any particular woman, and lost to the world. The fire had burned down to a glow of embers, and starshine lay over the high country. Out on the holding ground the latest gather was giving the night guard no trouble. Off to the southwest was the secret he had uncovered that day —Baine's so-called homestead.

He had been on the point of telling the men about this at suppertime, then he had decided to wait. He owed it to them to warn them, yet he knew that doing so would light a fuse. He hoped that Baine and his backers had been given at least passing pause. Jinx was bound to tell them of catching him in the act of ferreting out the secret. His doing so had robbed them of the advantage of surprise, which they seemed to have tried to gain.

Pace grew aware that more than bad dreams had disturbed his shallow sleep. Bim was walking in from the night band. He must have been checking on the herd, making some sound as he rode by coming back in. Pace felt a stab of worry. It wasn't usually necessary for the ramrod to do that at night. He pulled on his boots and climbed to his feet. He met Bim outside of camp.

"What's wrong with the critters?" he asked.

"I wasn't at the herd," Bim said gruffly. "I was just moseying around."

"Why?"

Bim halted and stared at him. "Look. I didn't feel like sleeping, so I took a little ride."

"You been up in the hills?" Pace insisted.

84

"Kee-rlst. Not long ago she wasn't good enough. You jealous of her, now?"

Stung, Pace said weakly, "I don't like you poking around alone at a time like this."

"Look who's talking!" Bim said with a hoot.

He went on to camp, but he went to the fire instead of to his bed and poured himself coffee from the pot that hung there day and night. Pace followed, unaccountably angry while understanding that Bim had a right to feel as he did. He fought to get hold of himself.

Bim realized that they were close to trouble, when they had an oversupply of it as it was. Speaking in an undertone, he said more moderately, "All right. It wasn't Jinx I went to see or even Wendy. I tried to talk to Spud."

"Talk to him?"

"He wouldn't let me."

Pace motioned with his head. "Come on. I've got something to tell you."

He walked out beyond earshot of the sleeping men. Bim followed, making it plain that he still had his back up. Pace told him of his discovery that day, omitting only his encounter with Jinx.

"That's what scared me," he explained. "I should have told you sooner. If you'd run into some of that bunch up there—"

"I didn't," Bim cut in. "If I had, I can take care of myself. I wish you'd get that through your head."

"I'm trying." Pace tried to grin.

Bim wanted no peace offering. He swung and went back into the camp and to his bed. When Pace followed, Bim didn't even look his way.

Pace made a smoke and consumed it before he turned in. He knew Bim would leave it to him whether to tell the crew. From outward appearances, at least, Bim's sympathies still lay with the nesters, including the Renners. An attack by the ranch was the last thing he wanted. But he, too, knew how tired the men were of it, how quickly they would take matters into their own hands if pushed too far.

Pace returned to his blankets to find that Jinx had tired of invading his dreams. Before he knew it he came awake to the cook's rousing yell.

"Rise and shine!"

It was a scene Pace had witnessed many times and always with satisfaction until that morning. The men, clapping on hats and pulling on boots, were whiskery and frayed and sullen. They needed an outlet for their edgy truculence or they would be at each other's throats. He doubted that he could tell them about the new danger and hold them in. Bim surprised him by taking over, himself.

"Been a new card dealt us, boys," Bim said when he issued day orders. He glanced briefly at Pace. After only a questioning second, which brought nothing from Pace, he went on. "Les Baine has set up a camp above the Cobble and Sand Creek forks. Whatever for, it's sure-fire he'll have a bunch of his owlhoot cronies hanging around. Do your work but watch your backs. Don't let yourselves be baited into a deadfall, like Cob Durnbo did."

They stared at Bim and then at each other with darkening faces. Then Charley Varley wheeled on Pace. "Why in hell," he demanded, "do we always have to give them sons of bitches the first jump?"

Pace bristled instinctively. None of them had dared to speak to him so angrily, so critically, before. He flung a glance at Bim, who was watching, waiting, seeming to relish the fact that he had struck a match in a powder house. It was unbelievable, considering his sentiments about the hill people.

"That's what I want to know," Lafe Loving added to Varley's outburst. "Cob was killed. They stampeded us on Baldy Slope. They've threatened our water. We got to wait till we've been gutted before we clean out them hills?"

Other heads nodded agreement, the regulars, the new hands, all of them. Pace knew that unless he handled this right they would either take matters into their own hands or leave him without a crew. Pulling rank wouldn't work at a time like this. If he owned a dozen Bedrocks, they would feel and act the same. But he couldn't justify his reasons without revealing that a powerful, personal vengeance in one man underlay the whole thing.

"We don't have cause to clean out the hills, Lafe," he said, with a mildness he was far from feeling. "We won't have one unless we lose our heads and do something to rally the nesters around the real snakes up there."

"How much does it take," Loving retorted, "before we go up there and clean out the real snakes? Man, you expect a day's work out of us. And for us to do it with none of us knowing when we're gonna get what Cob got."

"Of which," somebody muttered, "I've had a bellyful."

Another voice said, "Me, too."

"I know," Pace agreed. "And so have I. But only one man, with a few sidewinders supporting him, is responsible for what's going on. And I've got to say what I've been saying to you. Till they give us reason to deal with them,

86

without starting the range war they want to cover themselves with, our hands are tied. So far they haven't given us reason. When they do, they'll be taken care of. I promise you all that."

It was the most humble and forthright he had ever been with them, and the men were listening. Swede O'Brien was nodding his shaggy head. He was respected and well liked. Some seemed to agree with him, and the stubborn dissenters shrugged and lapsed into silence. Bim seized the moment to issue the day orders, and presently the outfit was scattering to its tasks.

Bim lingered behind. After an awkward moment, he said, "What they needed most was a chance to let off steam to you, personally. You never gave them one. I had to make one."

Pace stared at him, surprised at Bim's astuteness and skill in handling his men. "Do you think that will hold them in?" he asked.

"A while, I hope. At least till something else pops out of the box."

"It's pretty apt to."

"Yeah."

They stared at each other, then Bim rode off to join the men.

Moments later Pace set out on his own daily rounds. He found nothing wrong on Bear Prairie, but he had hardly sighted the Split Rock tanks on Baldy Slope, when he knew something was out of the way there. Froggy Jorgensen was camped there with one of the new men sent out by Dollar. Even at a distance Pace could see that Jorgensen had a rifle on his arm and was watching intently to make sure of the oncomer's identity. Pace waved his arm over his head and increased the speed of his horse.

"Am I glad to see you," Jorgensen said, when Pace drew up at the camp. "I would have rode down to get you, but I was afraid to leave the tanks. Paddy's missing. I don't know how long it's been. He was supposed to roust me out to relieve him at two o'clock. He didn't, and I never woke up till daylight. Him and his horse was gone."

Pace swung down. Paddy Olson had been one of the best of the new men and the only one who, in a checkered past, had had experience with cattle. "You got to know him better than I did," he reflected. "Would he be fool enough to let himself be lured off by something without rousing you first?" Jorgensen shook his head. "Then he cleared out. Nobody could have jumped him here at the tanks without it waking you up."

"But his soogans and war bag's still here. No drifter would light his shuck and leave his kit behind."

Pace had to agree. He regarded the tanks, which were a couple of narrow ponds fed by springs. "Anything drunk there since you've been up?" he asked.

"I been shooing the critters away. Doubt that anything was in to water before daylight. But now we don't know if that water's fit to drink. Have to drain off the tanks and let 'em fill up fresh."

"There's a way to find out."

Pace walked to the water, scooped up a cupped handful and, in spite of Jorgensen's yell of protest, drank it.

Jorgensen breathed, "You lost your mind?"

"Strychnine's bitter. For them to put enough in there to kill even a calf, you'd be able to taste it, I'd say. That water's sweet as the springs. Try it."

"Not me." Jorgensen stepped back.

"Let the critters drink it. I'll send one of the boys out to take Olson's place."

Jorgensen wasn't entirely reassured, nor was Pace when he headed on for Kettle Wells. Another thing Olson had left behind, if he had got itchy-footed, was the pay to his credit on the books. If he hadn't been subjected to actual violence, something had boogered him into flight. Yet there could be another explanation, Pace realized. In spite of his care to prevent such a thing, Olson might have been planted on him, instructed to desert at a propitious moment by simply vanishing into thin air. An outfit already jumpy would be powerfully disturbed by a man mysteriously vanishing from their midst.

This squared with the kind of cunning the ringleaders in the hills had been displaying, and Pace was pretty sure it was the real explanation. If so, Olson had been promised more money than he had earned as a water guard and the worth of the personals he had left behind. He would have to prove he had earned it before he could collect, and he would have to go into the backlands to get it.

He had to make sure of this, Pace knew, before he could hope to offset its spooky effect on the rest of his men. If he merely offered it as his opinion, they would regard it as shrugging off his responsibility, for Olson might well be in serious trouble. If he was, he was entitled to all the help his outfit could give him.

Pace checked Kettle Wells and found nothing out of the ordinary. The change was in his own mind. Both of the guards there were new men, and he found himself regarding them with suspicion. If one or both of *them* vanished, it would build up a pressure that nothing could restrain. He was of a mind to let all the new hands go at once and take his chances on the threat to the water. But he soon saw the futility of this. If he began to distrust every man on the payroll, the ranch would come apart without outside help.

He had to find Paddy Olson, whether he was a traitor or sorely in need of help.

Riding back toward the roundup camp, he followed the edge of the hills. The sun by then rode above and beyond the hills, so that he moved in shadow flung down by long stretches of rim. The lack of sharp light forced him to watch intently for fresh horse sign. If it was there somewhere, he would cut it, for the camp for which Olson had vanished was well off to his right.

He found sign sooner and easier then he had expected. At the draw of an old wash, he saw the open tracks of a horse ridden by a man both unhurried and unworried. Swinging down, Pace made sure they had been laid there not too long before. Then he backtracked them until he was satisfied that they came on a beeline from where he judged the Split Rock camp to be. They could have been made by someone beside Olson but, under the circumstances, Pace dismissed that chance. It had to be Olson, alone and leaving voluntarily. He wouldn't be heading into outlaw country if he thought he'd be harmed in any way when he got there.

His slight worry about the man's welfare removed, Pace felt anger build. He could respect the cleverness of the scheme but not the treachery of a man he had misjudged and trusted. He rolled a cigarette and smoked it, standing by his horse and considering his next move.

The country the wash led into was all strange to him. He could rack around in it for hours, even following a fairly warm trail, and wind up with nothing at all. Mounting, he continued to prove out his theory while he kept on along Olson's backtrail. The sign was fairly easy to follow until he was in sight of the Split Rock camp. From there on, Olson had been tricky. He had fouled sign until he was far enough out from camp to be hard to pick up. Pace didn't bother to ferret it out but rode straight in.

Cattle were drinking, now, at the tanks. Jorgensen was letting them come in and was himself in view. The puncher still looked worried when Pace rode up to him.

"Didn't expect you back this way," he said. "Something wrong at Kettle Wells?"

Pace shook his head. "Forget the tanks a while and get your horse. I need a witness."

Jorgensen looked puzzled but shrugged his shoulders. His horse was picketed on the meadow fed by the underground water. He saddled and rode out obediently with Pace. When they came to the place where Olson's trail grew plain, Pace pointed it out.

"That's what happened to Paddy Olson. Nobody had a twist on his tail. He headed into the back country on his own."

"What in tarnation for?"

"I reckon," Pace said wryly, "it was to collect for his services."

"He's working for that hill bunch?" Jorgensen swallowed. He had been campmates with the traitor for quite a while. "What doing?"

"Well, he had plenty of chances to ruin the water here, but he didn't. I never was sure they wanted anything but to pester us. His disappearance was to point out to the rest of you boys that the same thing could happen to you. It spooked *you*, didn't it?"

"It wasn't any comfort."

"And it might decide the newer men to clear out while they can. Come on. I want you to see for yourself where he went."

The puncher eyed the distant hills uneasily. "I'll take your word for that."

But he kept on with Pace, firsthand evidence of the potency of Tex Gilgen's new medicine.

90

CHAPTER 13

When Pace saw the excitement at the branding camp, he dug in his spurs. It was well past the noon hour, yet the entire crew was still there. He saw that some of them were looking his way, as though they had been waiting for him to get back. They formed about him even before he had swung down from his horse.

Bim stood slightly apart, dark-countenanced and grim. Pace wondered if, in spite of the morning's success in holding the men in, the boy had a mutiny on his hands. There was a bristling look to them all.

Whatever it was, Pace sensed that it was no time for the persuasion he had used that morning. He swept his eyes over them and snapped, "What are you men hanging around camp for? There's work to be done."

Lafe Loving shoved his thumbs under his belt and hunched his shoulders. "We ain't doing another lick of it," he announced, "till we've got them bastards off our backs."

Loving had been one of those left unmollified that morning. He had kept on stewing about it, building up the ferment in the others again. Or maybe Olson wasn't the only traitor planted in the outfit. Whatever, the roundup had been brought to a standstill. Most of the men looked like they would back Loving's ultimatum. If he ignored it, they would draw their time, paralyzing the ranch indefinitely.

Swede O'Brien, who had been standing in a dark study, lifted his head. "I know how you feel, Lafe," he said quietly. "But you ain't talking for me."

He walked over to stand beside Bim. Charley Varley nodded his head and joined them. So did several others, two of them men who had signed on only that spring. But a good half of them stayed with Loving.

"All right, Lafe," Pace said. "You and the men you've got so stirred up can have your time."

"Now, see here—!" Loving looked in consternation toward Varley and O'Brien. They were old saddlemates whose support he had counted on, and he had been surprised. Then he tossed his head in anger and said no more.

"You can draw your money at the bank, day after tomorrow," Pace snapped. "Get riding."

Bim watched in dismay. Loving swung on his heels. One or two of his supporters looked hesitant, then they followed him. Pace felt a touch of sorrow he couldn't indulge. In their lights, they had put up with enough, and it was time to think of their own skins. They began to roll their beds, which were their property. A couple of them looked like they would welcome a way to save face and stay on. But Loving's pride had been offended, and he held them. They shouldered their soogans and headed for the *remuda* to get their private horses.

Pace turned his attention to the men who had stuck and said, "Thanks, boys."

They were too worried to be gratified. "We'll be from now to Christmas," Bim said, shaking his head, "just winding up the branding."

"No, we won't. We'll bring in the water guards."

O'Brien said in disbelief, "And leave the water open?"

"Just that. If I'm right—and maybe I'm not—they've worked that angle for all they wanted out of it. It forced us to put on a bunch of extra men. Now they're out to strip us of them and more men, besides." He told them about Olson, and how he had proved that the man's disappearance had been strictly voluntary. "That's why I had to get rid of Lafe. I'd sooner fire the spooky ones that left with him than have them run out on us or maybe sell us out."

They seemed to agree with him, handicapped though it had made them. Much as he had been weakened, Pace had a feeling that his outfit had been drawn more tightly together. The men, as it were, had been separated from the boys. He told them to skip the afternoon circle and work the morning's gather. By another morning he would have a full crew again. The five Joe Dollar men still on the tanks were green as new hides at cattle work. Maybe another of them was of Olson's stripe. But with seasoned men to keep an eye on them, they could turn out the work.

It took the rest of the day to get the crew replacements and their camps moved to Pistol Peak. As he went about the job, Pace had a feeling that amused eyes were watching from some rim. It built up his impatience until he could hardly restrain it. He was leaving Baldy Slope and Bear Prairie wide open. It was a desperate gamble, but it might tempt the schemers into a move so clear-cut in origin and intent he could strike back with all he had at the real enemies—Gilgen, Renner and Baine. Himself against those

92

three. That was the only war here and the only excuse for one.

After supper, Pace rode down to ranch headquarters to make up the payroll on the men he had let go that day. He intended to send it on to the bank in Rowel the next morning by Calhoun, but the old man was nowhere in evidence. His personals were in the bunkhouse, but the nag he had ridden in on, back there, was gone. There had been no fire in the cookhouse stove at suppertime.

Pace was more annoyed than worried about it. He had an idea that with nobody around to watch him, the old codger had sneaked off to town. He was garrulous, liked to warm his bones with a few drinks, and in spite of his years had an eye for the women. So, Pace realized, he would have to stay overnight and take the payroll in, himself, to make sure it reached the bank. He would peel the old man's hide when he saw him again for deserting his post.

He put up his horse and went on to the big house. There was about an hour left of daylight, and he decided he had earned himself a bath and clean clothes. The house had the only real bathtub in the country, but he didn't want to bother heating water. He got a towel, soap and clean clothes and went down to the creek. He swam and splashed around awhile to cool off and forget his troubles. Then he soaped up and began to feel like a civilized man. Dressed again, he went up to the house's back porch and shaved for the first time in days.

Afterward, he lit a lamp and figured up the time of the men who had failed him. It would take a bite out of his bank account. The regular hands mostly let their pay ride except for spending money, and he had hired twice the usual number of extras that summer. If, later, he had to hire hayers and woodcutters—but he dismissed that prospect. He had more than a bank account to worry about.

He was about finished with the job when he heard a rap on the front door. It would be Calhoun, who apparently hadn't taken French leave after all. Relieved that he would be spared a ride to town, Pace called, "Come on in."

He had left the main door opened. He saw the screen swing out and blinked his eyes. Jinx Renner stepped in. She wore a blouse, short riding skirt and boots. A boy-sized hat rode pertly aslant on her dark hair. In spite of himself, he was captivated by the picture she made there.

As if she didn't know that all too well.

"Oh, it's you," she said, without a sign of surprise. She walked boldly across the living room and almost to his desk.

93

"I thought it was that nice old man. I was going to ask him if a bone-tired girl could rest herself here again."

"You saw Calhoun in town," Pace retorted. "When you noticed a light in the house you knew who was here."

Her mouth dropped open in a mock gasp. "Why, you're all but saying I'd ask *you* a favor like that."

"Why not? You'd be as safe with me as with old Cal."

She lowered her eyes demurely. "But I'm scared you wouldn't be as safe as Cal'd be."

"I'll take my chances. And I'll put up your horse."

She had expected to tease him again then go cheerily on her way. He had called her bluff, and for the first time in his experience with her she was disconcerted. He got up from the desk. She stepped back, although they were still separated by a stretch of floor.

She said hastily, "No, I've got to go on."

"Time enough for that come morning. And if you relied on that stingy gun to let you get away with this, don't forget. You couldn't bring yourself to use it on me, up there in the hills."

She remembered that. She looked hastily toward the door then back at his eyes. They told her that for once she had baited a man she couldn't handle, and it had her rattled. For an instant she seemed frightened and vulnerable, then her jaw set. She tried to cut past and beat him out to her horse. He caught her arm and flung her around so fast she nearly fell.

"No, by God. You invited yourself here and here you stay till I tell you to leave." He pushed her toward a chair. "Set down and make yourself to home."

"If you molest me," she breathed, "my brother will kill you."

"He's already tried, and he'll keep trying till I kill him. And it's time some man gave you what you've been begging for all your grown life."

She sat down. He thought it was more from weakness than in obedience. Her cheeks had drained of color. "Let me go," she whispered. "Please?"

He went over to the fireplace mantel and got himself a cigar. He took his time lighting it. "Maybe I could be bought off, though," he said finally.

"I can't give you any information. They don't tell me very much."

"I know. They let you rack around looking for a different kind of trouble that you've got yourself into, finally. I know all I need to know about them and their intentions. I've got information for you to take to Howie and Gilgen. Promise

94

to do it, and I might let you board your horse and go home."

She looked baffled. Her vanity was such that she found it hard to believe he had anything but her charms in mind. He had them in mind and had had since the night she danced with him in Rowel. But he had other things that, at least for the time being, were more important. If they could sow dissention and distrust in his outfit, he could do the same among the ringleaders in the hills. And, in her caprice, she had brought him a way to do it.

Jinx said meekly, "All right. What do you want me to tell them?"

"They won't like it, but it's something they ought to know. They're putting too much stock in Les Baine. They'll be surprised to hear that Baine approached me, a while back in Rowel. He offered to switch sides, just like that, for the right price."

Jinx's eyes had rounded. "You're making it up?"

"He did, and I told him where to go. But that's not the reason he's still with them, or why he's set himself up in that war camp. The only side he's on or ever intended to be on is Les Baine's. Howie and Gilgen can't trust him anymore than I could. He's using them instead of them using him. Baine aims to make himself top dog in this ruckus."

She eyed him suspiciously. "They won't believe it. I don't know if I do."

"All right. I'll put your horse in the corral."

"No! I'll tell them!"

He smiled. "Going to tell them how you happened to learn?"

She dropped her gaze to the floor. "I'll say I run into you on the trail."

"All right. Get riding. I've got no further interest in you."

Her eyes darkened, and she tossed her head. But she said nothing and rose to her feet. Oddly, in that gesture of defiance, she looked more desirable than ever. He followed her to the yard and her horse.

She didn't show her true spirit until she had mounted and knew she could get away from him. Then she said heavily, "I'll keep my promise, but not to do you any good turn. I never hated anybody in my life the way I hate you, and I've hated a few something fierce. The next time I'll do the laughing. Don't say I didn't warn you."

She dug in her heels and was gone into the night.

He returned to his payroll and finished it, finding it hard to keep his mind on the figures. It wasn't all because she had given new life to the thoughts that had plagued his mind

95

and insinuated themselves into his dreams. What disturbed him was that she had turned out to be a more complicated girl than he had supposed. She had depth beyond that of a fetching flirt. She had convinced him of an integrity he hadn't conceded her before. He had really scared her, and he had scared her that night in the woods at Silver Butte. Yet something about him kept challenging her to the good of neither of them.

At least she had furnished him with a way to work on Gilgen's and Renner's nerves, the way they had worn his own raw and hair-triggered. Hopefully, it could put that bunch at each other's throats. Whether or not they believed what he had told Jinx, they couldn't help but regard Baine, thereafter, with suspicion. Prying them apart even that much would help. If he could find some way to snake Spud Stevens and Wendy out of the situation, he would have come a ways toward offsetting the damage he had suffered at their hands. But he had tried everything he could think of with Spud, and Wendy, also, without success.

He rose the next morning to see, when he looked out his bedroom window, that smoke was drifting up from the cookhouse chimney. Calhoun was back and probably shaking in his boots, for he would have seen the extra horse in the corral. Pace dressed and went over there, hoping to find the codger in shape to be sent back to town with the payroll. He wanted to get back to the roundup, himself.

Calhoun was sitting at the big table, drinking coffee, when Pace walked in on him. At least his hands were steady, and he looked clear-eyed.

"Have a good time in town, Cal?" Pace asked.

"Go ahead and peel my hide." Calhoun put down his cup. "But it's a good thing I went in. I seen Lafe Loving. He'd had time to cool off, and he asked me to tell you something. I was going to ride up to the roundup till I seen your horse in the corral."

"Well, what did he have to say?"

"The men you sacked, along with Lafe, are going to throw in with the hill outfit. That is, after they collect what they got coming from you. They say you're too yellow to stand up and fight, and they aim to be on the winning side." Calhoun looked up at Pace's face. "Wait a minute. They're saying that, not me."

"Go on."

"That's about it. Lafe wanted you to know what they're doing. And that he's having no part of it, himself."

Pace nodded, and Calhoun rose to bring his breakfast. An extra handful of enemies, he reflected while he poured himself coffee, wouldn't make much difference. What bothered him was that those were men who had worked for him and changed sides because they thought he lacked courage.

He ate his breakfast, then went back to the big house to get the payroll, which he gave to Calhoun.

"You're in for another trip to town," he told the oldster. "If you see Lafe again, tell him all he's got to do is ride back with you."

Calhoun grinned. "I got a hunch he will. None of 'em expected to get his walking papers that fast."

Pace saddled and headed for the summer range.

CHAPTER 14

Pace sat his horse on a shoulder of Pistol Peak, itself, watching the scene below him. The cattle converging on the flat down there, were the last to be gathered in the spring roundup. When they had been worked and thrown back on the range, he would have brought off what had seemed so desperately uncertain for so long. There was satisfaction in this but no real relief.

He must have hampered Gilgen with the information he sent through Jinx, a couple of weeks before. Les Baine, on the other hand, would have been handicapped because of the suspicions. But the only thing Pace could be sure of was that there had been no trouble from them, although he couldn't conclude from that that they had been stopped for long. If he had divided them, one side or the other would soon dominate. How he organized the work and the outfit for the rest of the summer had to take that into account.

He watched the various drives of cattle converging into a herd on the holding ground. For weeks he had kept his hands off that part of the work. While Bim did some things different to what he would have done, he had got results, and Pace could find no fault with the way he had handled it. Yet this restraint, and the painful restraint he had shown on behalf of the nesters, plus the apology he had once made to Bim for his former attitude toward Wendy Stevens —nothing had diminished the cool standoffishness in Bim.

Pace rode down from the high ground and cut across the flat to the camp. Bim was at the fires. He acknowledged his brother's arrival with no more than a glance and a nod. Pace beckoned him to the side.

"Tell the boys at supper," he said, "to draw lots for town. Half this coming weekend, the rest the next."

Bim's features brightened in spite of himself. The men had more than come through, and some of the green ones had turned into good cowhands. They needed and had earned recreation.

"You think it's smart to let so many go at once?" he asked.

Pace shrugged. "Who knows? But I think our hill neighbors are through with monkeyshines. We wouldn't take bait, in spite of all they did. They couldn't scare off enough men to hurt us. I don't think they'll waste more time on stuff like that."

"I wish we could count on it," Bim said tiredly. "There's a heap of summer work still ahead, then comes the beef gather and the fall drive."

"We're going to take the gamble," Pace told him. "We're running a ranch in spite of them, and we'll keep on doing that."

Bim said doubtfully, "We could be sorry."

"Maybe, but we'll be caught up with the work."

Bim didn't seem to hear him. He had turned his head to stare toward the Cobble Creek gap, and his features set themselves in a dark study. Pace swung around to see a rider coming from that direction toward them, the horse moving at a walking trot.

"What in tunket," Bim muttered, "is she coming here for?"

Pace's breath checked. "She?"

"That's a horse Wendy Stevens usually rides."

For an instant, Pace had had the unnerving feeling that the oncomer was Jinx. He hadn't forgotten her parting threat that unforgettable night. The oncoming rider was sure enough Wendy. Bim moved out to meet her. Pace wondered if he should give them privacy, then decided to follow.

Wendy reined in and let them come up to her. Her face had a hard set, and her eyes were narrowed. She looked only briefly at Bim, and with distaste, then turned her attention to Pace. His hope that she might be getting sense into her pretty head, finally, expired.

She said bitterly, "So you're done with your roundup."

"Just about," Pace said, puzzled. "Why?"

"Now you'll have the time to take care of us squatters."

"I reckon you know what you're talking about," Bim said angrily. "Mind letting us in on it?"

Wendy glanced at him. There was nothing in her eyes to confirm Pace's suspicion that she still cared something for Bim. She twisted in the saddle, a slim and yet exciting figure. She opened the flap of a saddle pocket and fished out a piece of paper. It was folded, but she opened it with a snap of the wrist.

"Here."

Bim looked at the thing and, with stunned eyes, handed

99

it to Pace. Wendy said sardonically, "He knows what it says."

Pace had only to read four words to know plenty: WARNING. GET OUT. NOW. There were torn tack holes in the corners, showing that Wendy had pulled it down from somewhere.

He lifted apprehensive eyes to Wendy's. Hers showed that she was convinced it was his doing. "Where did you get this?" he asked.

"Where do you suppose I got it?" she returned. "Every nester in the foothills had one of them stuck to his gatepost or barn door when he got up this morning. Don't try to tell me you don't know how they got there."

Pace knew how they had got there even better than she did. An attack on the nester colony, staged to look like the work of Bedrock ranch, would start a range war as effectively as if the ranch were guilty. Bim saw through it, too, for his lips were white and pinched.

The respite they had anticipated, only moments earlier, had been a sheer illusion.

"How could anybody get that close to your place," Pace asked her, "without setting off your hounds?"

She scowled, hesitated, then said, "They been moved up to the point over Sand and Cobble creeks."

"I know. To Les Baine's camp. But how could anybody from outside get past them? And then go around posting warnings everywhere without Baine knowing and investigating?"

She seemed puzzled for a moment, then said with a toss of her head, "There's other ways into the hills. You've used them before."

"If Baine's protecting you people like he claims," Pace persisted, "why hasn't he got guards and a sentry dog or so on all the ways in there?"

He was cutting the ground from under her hot-headed reasoning. She said weakly, "I don't know anything about that."

"Well, I can make some guesses about it," Pace assured her. "The ringleaders, up there, *want* a way left open. They weren't able to bait us into using it. But there's still got to be a way open we *could* have used. Don't you fall for it, Wendy. I don't think you have, entirely, or you wouldn't have ridden down here about it."

"I only come down to warn you," Wendy retorted, spirited again. "We've got protection. You'll only get people killed and hurt. You better think twice about it."

She started to swing her horse. Bim's hand shot out and

grabbed its bridle. The animal shied and tossed its head, but Bim's grip held. "Protection!" he snorted, looking up at her. "I think so highly of your protection I'm not letting you go back up there!"

She started to use her quirt on him, then her raised arm fell. "Why should you want to spare me?" she asked. "Anymore than the rest up there?"

Bim's cheeks colored. Pace cut in.

"Let go her bridle, Bim. She's got to play out her string the way she thinks she has to. It won't do any good to keep her from it. But I sure God hope, Wendy, that you and Spud have sense enough in your muleheads to sleep outside the pocket the next few nights. And not let anybody else, up there, know it."

Wendy gave him a queer, searching glance. Reluctantly, Bim loosened his grip on the bridle straps. She turned the horse and rode off.

Bim's eyes stayed on her. "They've made everything that's happened point a finger at Spud," he muttered. "That's who they'll hit. And you're letting her ride back into it."

"Not if she takes my tip," Pace said, "about being somewhere else when the lightning strikes. Spud, too, if she can make him listen. I eat every word I ever spoke against that girl."

"Why's that?"

"She said she come to warn us, and she did. She found a way to tell us what's shaping up without being disloyal to her kin and kind."

"By damn." For the first time in ages, Bim's eyes warmed to him. "I think maybe you're right."

Grim as the turn of events had been, Pace found his own spirits lifted. Wendy hadn't known he was aware of the power Baine had gathered to himself up there. That had been part of her warning. And she had managed to get across that Baine's bogus protection had swung most of the nester colony behind him. Pace wondered where this left Gilgen and Renner. It didn't much matter. The threat to the Bedrock was as great one way as it was the other.

"Well," Bim said, while they walked back to camp, "I guess that cancels town leave for the boys."

"Maybe not." Pace shook his head. "If they stage an attack on Stevens, or the whole nester settlement, it's got to look convincing. With half our outfit in Rowel celebrating the end of roundup, we wouldn't look very warlike, would we? Go ahead and tell the boys."

101

"We better not say what Wendy come down for. They must've noticed her."

That was certain. No girl, plain or pretty, could show up near a branding camp without being noticed plenty. Pace agreed that it would be better not to tell the men about the suspected plans. They had shaped up fine behind him, but there was no sense in putting too much strain on them.

Bim made the announcement when the crew, except for the herders, had gathered for supper. The men took it without the usual outburst of skylarking hilarity. They were bone-tired and badly in need of diversion, whatever form it would take for each. But the sense of crisis hadn't been dissipated with the successful completion of the calf branding. They knew there was more and maybe worse trouble to come.

Pace left camp right after supper, telling Bim he was going down to headquarters to make up another payroll to send to the bank. This one would provide the crew with spending money. Bim was to bring down the wagon and most of the crew as soon as this last gather was worked in the morning. Pace meant to do what he claimed, but he had something to do first that he didn't want to mention.

He followed the main trail down the basin until he was closed off from the cow camp. There he left the trail and headed west, cutting back on the far side of Pistol Peak. It was still light, and he wanted darkness before he continued on. He swung down at the peak, trailed reins, and rolled himself a cigarette.

An unaccustomed serenity came to him while he waited, disturbed only by a nagging awareness that it could be based on false hopes. The showdown still had to wait until the situation shook itself down, with only the right people involved in it. Holding to the end had been the heaviest burden that life and the Bedrock had ever placed on his shoulders. So far he had carried the load, and this brought him peace for the moment. But there were so many unforeseeable stumbling blocks ahead.

He waited there until night had settled over the foothills. Mounting, he climbed up into the pines, entering the rough country between himself and Silver Butte. He rode quietly, although the vicinity seemed as pristine as it had been when men first came to the Bedrock country. Occasionally he reined in to listen for a moment before he went on.

He had barely penetrated the hill country, itself, when he heard it, the bugling of a hound off ahead.

He stopped still with a grin ghosting on his mouth. He knew what he had come to make sure of as a result of

102

Wendy's queer visit to the branding camp. What he had pointed out to Wendy had resulted in the nesters demanding guards on this back approach to their country. Baine hadn't dared to refuse, and in consenting he had hamstrung himself. If a nester setup was attacked now, particularly the Stevens pocket, the ranch could be blamed for it only on the assumption that it had sprouted wings.

Heading back in the direction he had come from, Pace warned hmself not to make too much of it. The nesters, including Wendy and her father, didn't have to distrust the ringleaders up there, to take such a step. Taking it just made sure they weren't caught by surprise from any direction. That, Pace reflected, was a help to himself, but it didn't imply that he had won even Wendy over.

He passed the herd and camp at a distance and continued down the main basin trail. Headquarters was dark when he came to it, but Calhoun's nag was in the corral. Pace took care of his own horse, then went to the big house and directly to bed.

The roundup outfit reached home ground late the next afternoon. This was always a happy point in the season, and the men were beginning to show signs of a holiday spirit. They would all want to head for town as soon as they were squared away, for only those who had won in the drawing of lots had come down from the summer range. Old Cal watched the preparations with an expression so forlorn Pace told him to go, too. He would be there to tend store, himself, over the weekend.

Most of them were on their way before Pace noticed that Bim was making no preparations. "How come?" he asked. "You've had your nose to the grindstone as long as any of them."

Bim shook his head. "Don't feel like it."

Pace realized that he was too concerned for Wendy and her father to leave the ranch. He told him what he had discovered the night before, that the nesters didn't aim to be caught napping, no matter who had posted the warnings for them to clear out. Bim took a little heart from that but still didn't want to go to town. Pace gave the payroll to Froggy Jorgensen so the men could draw what they wanted at the bank the next morning.

It was like the old days, being alone with Bim that evening, but Bim didn't let it really be the same. He busied himself with the equipment that would be stored until the start of the beef gather. He had brought down the tally books, and Pace spread them on his desk and began to figure up the year's increase. Darkness drove Bim indoors, but Pace had lighted a lamp and he kept on working. He wasn't crowding Bim. If the boy wanted a conversation, he would start one. Bim didn't. Presently he went on up to his room.

Once again Pace was taken flatfooted when a voice, some time later, called through the screen door.

"That you, Pace? It's little old me again."

Pace felt as though the floor had fallen out from under his chair. Without a by your leave Jinx opened the screen and came in. She wasn't in town clothes, this time, but she looked just as devastating with her long legs in slim pants. He dared not look at her open-necked, tantalizingly filled shirt.

"I seen the outfit busting for town," Jinx said cheerily. "And I didn't want you to feel lonely."

Pace said quiety, "Go home, Jinx. It won't work!"

"Why?" she lifted her eyes and said, "Oh, I see. Evening, Bim. I thought you'd be off to cut loose your wolf, along with the boys."

Pace turned slowly, lifting dismayed eyes. Bim had come out of his room and was leaning over the balcony railing. He stared at Jinx, then cut angry eyes to Pace.

"Reckon I should have gone," he said. "I was nudged, but I didn't catch on."

Pace's face flushed with anger. Jinx couldn't have set things up better for her threatened revenge than he had done. Sending Calhoun to town. Urging Bim to go. She knew the men had brought in the wagon and then had gone to town. She had watched and knew damned well that Bim hadn't been with them.

"You had your little joke," he said heavily. "Now get the hell gone."

"Why, Pace!" She simpered in a mock pout. "You didn't act like this the other night when I was here. Or the time before when I stayed all night."

Pace flung a glance upward. He wished he hadn't, for it incriminated him completely. Bim swung on his heel and went back into his room.

Jinx said in a lowered voice, "Try and talk your way out of that, sweetie."

She turned and sauntered to the door. There she paused to look back and smile. A moment later Pace heard her horse leave, much less quietly than it had come in. One thing she hadn't distorted in the least. He would never be able to make Bim believe the truth. Jinx had had the last laugh she had sworn to have.

CHAPTER 15

Pace paused at Bim's closed door, then shook his head and went on to his own room. Calhoun could tell Bim who all had been at headquarters the night Jinx took it on herself to sleep there. But Cal wasn't there now, himself. Nor would Bim, in his present frame of mind, believe what had really happened on her later visit, as uninvited as the first. Maybe after he simmered down, he would listen to reason. Right now, reason was buried in his offended mind. Even if he was out from under Jinx's spell now, he'd never forget she was the second girl his brother had horned him away from.

Pace was undressing in the dark when he realized that Bim had been waiting for him to clear out of the downstairs. He heard the creak of treads and crossed to the window. A minute later Bim appeared below in the yard. He headed straight for the corral and probably was going back up to the summer range wanting no more of his brother's company. Pace stood there until Bim had ridden out, then went to bed.

He was lying in bed sleepless when his bad knee began to hurt. It came to him that this was the first time it had bothered him in several weeks. He had kept up his efforts to master the full use of the knee again. This had become so mechanical, it had slipped from his conscious mind. Once someone had accused him of using it to nurse a grudge against the nesters. He winced, remembering that this had been Jinx. The night he trapped himself into having to dance with her in Rowel.

Was it only coincidence that the improvement in the knee had jibed with his improving attitude toward that contingent in the hills? Even toward her in his slow learning that, whatever else she was, she was no cheap tramp? Of course it was mere chance. If a shot-up knee felt like hurting, it hurt, and that was the size of it.

There was no real need, but he was up at daybreak, both from habit and from the fitfulness of his sleep. Dressed, he went downstairs, forcing thoughts of what had happened

105

there the night before from his mind. Moving on to the cookshack, he started a fire, made coffee and fried flapjacks from the cook's sour dough crock. The food was tasteless and, afterward, so was the cigar he lighted. The nerves of his knee began to feel like red-hot wires.

Abruptly, he knew that Jinx, with her talk of grudges, had been barking up the right tree. But when she talked about nesters, she was after the wrong varmint. In spite of his disdainful treatment, he had lusted for her daily and nightly from the time he first held her in his arms to dance. Hating her now, he still lusted, and the compound was deadlier than his fading hatred of whoever had ruined his knee. For Jinx had ruined something even more valuable— his relationship with Bim.

He left the cookhouse figuring to finish up the bookwork while he had the place to himself. He was far too restless to be attracted to the job, but he forced himself to it. At noon he skipped eating, for the bad taste was still in his mouth. He felt a strong urge to ride up to the summer range, but now he felt as little inclined to see Bim as Bim did to see him. Anyway, if he had guessed wrong and there had been trouble up there, somebody would have been down to tell him by now.

It was early in the afternoon when he thought that this was happening. A beat of hoofs rose out of the vast silence. Pace shoved to his feet and rushed to a window to stare out perplexedly. The rider, whose horse was flattened in a dead run, was coming from the wrong direction—from toward town. He hurried to the yard and was standing there when Froggy Jorgensen pulled a sweat-streaked horse to a stop.

"Trouble in town!" Jorgensen said heavily. His always protuberant eyes were half popped from their sockets." Gun trouble—Bim and that sidewinder Baine!"

"Bim?" It was a stupid question. He had only assumed, the night before, that Bim had gone up to the summering cattle. "He's—?"

"Alive, but hit hard! The doc said for you to get there fast!"

"Where's he hit?"

Jorgensen tapped his chest, then went on in the breathless bursts of a man whose excited heart refused to slow down. "Baine baited him. It was something about you and—and Jinx Renner. Something dirty. None of us boys seen it. Baine managed to catch Bim where he had no help."

"Saddle my horse."

Pace swung and hurried back into the house, every nerve

106

in his body numb. He strapped on his gun rig and got his hat off the peg by the door. Baine had been set back in his ambitions by the nesters' refusal to be taken in completely. It had discouraged him from pulling off his own treacherous attack on some nester setup.

He couldn't have foreseen that Bim would be in town. But when he saw Bim there he had recognized the opportunity it offered him to recoup. Whether Bim lived or died, nothing now could stop the outfit from going after him and his confederates. Pace knew he would lead them, himself. And if Bim died—Pace tried to shake the thought from his head but it wouldn't dislodge. He would be as responsible as Baine. He had let the boy ride off in a state of ferment that he had helped to create, himself.

Jorgensen was waiting in the yard with a saddled horse. He wanted to return to town, but Pace told him to stay there and keep an eye on things. He swung into the saddle and drove his spurs in hard.

He had never covered the distance to Rowel so fast, yet it seemed that it had never taken him so long. He didn't think about anything much, and his body stayed cold and unfeeling. Yet when the town lay below him at the river's edge he thawed out to feel a sick dread. Hours had passed since Jorgensen left for the ranch. Much could have happened since then.

The street, when he rode onto its dirty stretch, showed him nothing but its usual jam-packed, hurly-burly scene. Yet he grew aware of tension before he had ridden a block. A shooting, whether or not a killing, could polarize the rawest of towns, supplying a new focus of interest, creating an expectancy, an excited waiting. He didn't know most of them, but somebody who recognized him must have sent word of his arrival rippling along the walks. Eyes turned toward him. Men spoke to each other.

It must be that Baine was still in town, safe in his protest of self-defense, basking in his latest glory.

In the second block Pace saw O'Brien step from the crowd onto the street to wave him down. Pace stopped out in the street to draw him out of earshot of the curious throng.

Pace said quietly, "How is he?"

"Holding on."

"Where is he?"

"Room in a fleabag hotel, down the street there. It was closest to where it happened. They'd took him there before any of us heard about it. Now they say he can't be moved. Not now, anyhow."

"Is he conscious?"

"Off and on."

Pace turned into the next empty tying space, O'Brien walking beside the horse, and swung down. His knee, when his weight came onto it, started to hurt like blazes. That little memento from his enemies, and now Bim gunned down, hating him because of what Jinx had done.

The shooting took place on the street in front of Dollar's saloon, O'Brien was telling him. Baine had stopped Bim and said something to him. The only witness who knew Bim said it had to do with his brother's making time with his old girl. Bim could have been pretty likkered. At least he had smelled of booze later and had looked kind of wild when O'Brien saw him just before it happened. Or Bim forgot Baine's reputation. At least he reached and was shot before he got off a shot of his own.

Every bitter passion known to men was in O'Brien's seamy face. "But Bim reached first. According to the witnesses, there was no question about it. Baine's clean as a hound's tooth with the law."

"He still around?" Pace asked.

"I think so. Hank Alper keeps a deputy here. Deputy asked a few questions. That was it."

Pace asked the dreaded question. "What does the doc think?"

"His name's Tryon. I talked to him, but he didn't hold out much hope. Baine's slug went clear through the chest. Tryon said it hangs on how much damage was done in there. He looks in pretty often, but he's contract doctor for the railroad and a busy man. Us boys been taking turns, the rest of the time, setting with Bim and keeping him as comfortable as we can."

They had reached the hotel. Its entrance was only an unswept set of stairs rising between a mercantile and one of the countless saloons. There was a window in the wall at the top of the stairs, but it was shut. A door just beyond opened and a girl looked out and smiled. Her face went wooden when she saw Pace's eyes, and she shut the door quickly. The air swam with heat and the smell of people. O'Brien stopped a couple of doors farther on.

"If he's awake," the puncher said quietly, "don't ask him questions. The doc don't want him to talk."

Pace nodded, and O'Brien opened the door. Charley Varley, who had been standing by the one window for air, swung around. Pace nodded to him, then let his eyes shift to the battered iron bedstead. A worn blanket had been thrown back over the foot of the bed. Bim lay there naked

108

because of the heat, his chest swaddled in white bandage that seemed the only clean thing in the room. There was no visible bloodstain, which meant nothing. A puncture wound did its bleeding where it did more damage. The chest rose and fell to a fast, shallow breath. But there was no rattle in the breathing, not yet.

Pace moved nearer. Bim's eyes were closed, whether in unconsciousness or sleep. At a motion of Pace's hands, the punchers left the room, and he sat down in the chair at the head of the bed.

"The hell of it is," he said softly, "there wasn't a thing to all that."

Bim didn't respond. No muscle moved. There was no change in his breathing. Pace didn't try to reach him again. But he sat there a long time thinking of all the years since Bim had been left in his care. A care he hadn't been able to terminate, although Bim became a man, and still could not end.

He had to do something about it all, and yet he felt wholly helpless.

He wasn't aware of time having passed but suddenly he came back to the moment to see the door open quietly. A man in a frock coat came in. The black bag he carried told who he was. He nodded, saying nothing. Pace climbed to his feet to let the doctor have the chair. Tryon took it and felt Bim's brow, listened to his chest, and held his wrist for a long moment. He still said nothing. Pace couldn't say anything. They stared at each other. Then Tryon shrugged. It said everything.

"Heart's good," he said. "He's young." He rose and offered his hand. "Anyone could tell you're his brother."

Pace took the hand. The man's grip was strong. He was doing all he could with the little he had to work with in this primitive helltown. Tryon closed the bag, picked it up and left. O'Brien looked in, but Pace shook his head, and the puncher closed the door instead of coming in.

Again it was waiting, and Pace saw by the window that the light was softening, out there. Bad as the day had been, he hated to see it end. Night held its own terrors, even if they were only in a man's mind. Pain sharpened in darkness. Life seemed so much more tenuous then. He thought about Baine, who had delivered the insult to Bim with clearly evident intent. Of Baine who, while not his main enemy, had become Gilgen and Renner's striking arm.

Hearing movement behind him, Pace swung around. Bim had turned over in bed and was staring toward him. His eyes had an expression that kept Pace from moving nearer.

Bim's tongue wet his dry lips. He said in a weak, frayed voice, "Get outta here."

Stupefied, Pace stammered, "The doc don't want you to talk, right now." Certainly not to say what Bim had just said.

"Damn you—beat it! You hear?"

Anger flushed Bim's cheeks. Pace knew if he tried to square matters just then, it would lead to dangerous extremes. He nodded his head in submission. His feet felt like millstones while he moved to the door and went out. He nodded dumbly to Varley, who went into the room. The hot hallway smelled vile. He felt dizzy and sick. Bim believed whatever Baine had taunted him about, however much he had resented Baine's saying it. If he died, he would have died believing it forever.

He nearly turned back to make Bim listen. But it wouldn't do to excite the boy more than he was already. Pace moved along the hallway and descended the dirty stairs. The walks were more crowded than ever. The construction hands, their work over, their suppers put away, were starting their various searches for the other rewards of the night. Cards. Talk. Booze. Women. All the pleasures of sense for which they drove their bodies through the long, hot days. Aimless. Yet as well off, at the end, as a man who drove himself relentlessly with a single aim.

He thought of Arliss, struck by the fact that she had scarcely entered his thoughts since the last time he was in town. Jinx, tool of the serpent, had driven her out. He didn't want to see Arliss, not now, yet he knew he should. She was sanity and decency, a bit of gentleness in a vicious world, a touch of beauty in an ugly world. He found himself moving through the throng toward the Fandango.

And then he saw Les Baine.

The man came along the opposite sidewalk, oddly clearing room for himself by his mere passing. He walked with an arrogance, an awareness of the awe he had so newly created. And a smugness. Whether Bim died or lived, Baine had kept himself untouchable by the law, except by the law of the gun. His own vaunted gun rode his hip boldly, maybe soon to receive a bright new notch.

While Pace had halted to stare, Baine seemed to have no awareness of him. Yet he must have, for other men did, all of those close enough to be aware of the proximity. They were still, watchful, some fearful, for a few were ducking into nearby doorways. Pace waited for Baine to turn his head, but Baine didn't do so, passing on by. Pace

110

watched until the man had turned into a saloon at the end of the block. He saw the disappointment in the eyes around him.

He went on to the Fandango. Arliss was downstairs. She looked at him with grave eyes, not speaking, and turned and let him follow her into her office under the inside stairs. She shut the door, then motioned him into a chair. He was too keyed up to sit still, to talk. He didn't know why he had come there.

She was searching his face with troubled eyes. He wondered if she had heard how Baine had goaded Bim into going for his gun. The lie that Bim believed, that she might believe, too.

"It's horrible," she said, at last. "I wanted Bim brought to my rooms so I could take care of him. By the time I heard of it, it was too late. They'd taken him to that awful hotel. I can't go there."

Pace nodded. Of course she couldn't. It had nearly turned his own stomach, leaving out of account the girls who waited at the head of the stairs. He studied her face and remembered the bruise that had been there on his previous visit. It had cleared up. Instead of marked, it was a tired face, now.

"There's nothing anybody can do," he said. "Even Tryon's waiting to see."

"I know. Pace?" She hesitated. "Are you looking for Baine?"

He let his eyes rest on her, but it brought him no peace. The currents that ran in her were as mystifying as they had ever been. She would never let him know and truly understand them. She spoke with him, shared this grave moment with him, without really coming out of her cover.

He remembered her question and said, "I don't know. I seen him. I think he seen me. He passed me by. I let him. The next time—?" He shrugged his shoulders.

"He's waiting for you to brace him. He has to. And if you do, he'll kill you. I couldn't bear that." She came up close to him, slid her hands under his arms and pressed her face to his chest. "I want you. When Bim's out of danger, I'll come to the ranch." She pressed closer. "Be there. Promise?"

"Don't tie me with offers. I'll make you no promises."

She said nothing. He left.

111

CHAPTER 16

His knee smoldered like a fire log, but his walk was paced, steady. Coming out of the Fandango, he had realized what had carried him beyond the wanting of a woman. It was something as primitive as that, as fundamental. It was the only thing that would put at rest the foment in him.

He went into Dollar's saloon, but Baine wasn't there. Nor was he on the street, or in any of the half-dozen other dives Pace entered. But the search would have its own effect. Men watched and word traveled. Soon Baine would hear of it and make himself available, his nostrils flared with a lust greater than for a woman. A lust such as he, himself, felt now.

He walked to the end of the street and waited, drawing on a cigar. He had spoken to no one, voiced nothing. He could have been no more than a restless man waiting out the crisis that had been visited on his brother. Yet the town read it the way the town wanted it to be. The way it had to be. He pulled on the cigar until the first ashes fell, then dropped it into the dust.

He was nearly to the fleabag hotel, where Bim lay, when Baine appeared on the street ahead of him, emerged from the stairs of another second-floor fleshpot. Baine halted, staring, and it dawned on Pace that, for once, the man had been taken by surprise. Baine must have been amusing himself in some upstairs room and hadn't yet heard that he had another chance to shine.

He recovered quickly and pulled a look of amusement onto his face. The amusement was less than convincing. He was disconcerted, confronted with a situation he hadn't arranged himself.

"Don't look at me that way, Larabee," he said in mock reproof. His eyes searched the street. As big a gallery as he could have asked for had pressed in as close as it dared to come. "I reckon I know how you feel about your brother. But is a man supposed to hold still and let a fool kid blow his head off?"

"You call yourself a man?" Pace, too, spoke to the gallery, for it could be as effective on a man like Baine as a gun. "What I see's a bully trapped by his reputation in a situation he didn't get to set up himself. It's got you rattled, hasn't it, Baine? You've got to meet it because people are watching, and somehow you're not sure of the odds."

"Now, look here!" Baine said heavily. "Nobody talks to me like that and lives!"

Pace said softly, "Threatening me, Baine?"

"I'm telling you, but I'm giving you a chance! Make your move!"

"Hah."

"Hear me? Make your move, or I'm gonna drill you through the guts! I'm gonna send you up to die with your brother!" A sound came from somewhere, like a concerted gasp. Baine heard it and it encouraged him. "He's a better man than you, you hen-house weasel! He tried to stand up for you, even after you took his gal! He's got you beat by a mile!"

"True," Pace said.

Baine stared, speechless. He had hoped to make his baiting work for him, and it hadn't. For the first time, he was at a loss.

It was a sound from the gallery that triggered him, somebody's moving to cover, maybe. Baine's hand moved, and Pace wasn't the only one to see it. Pace was aware, too, of pain in his knee, and then he reacted.

He felt his hand moving, the fingers spreading and bunching, with his eyes never swerving. Even as Baine's gun whipped up, he felt the action of his own trigger finger. He fired from the hip even as he saw the flash and heard the roar of the other gun. He felt something tick his shirt and burn across his side.

A look of astonishment grew on Baine's twisting face as he staggered back, lost the use of his legs and fell. He had nearly made the threatened gut shot, but he wasn't going to get a second chance. The bullet that had prevented it had torn into the center of his chest. He had only enough life left in him to twitch his legs. Then he was motionless, a toppled idol, sprawled on the splintered planks.

Eyes all about stared disbelievingly. Quickly word spread along the walks in either direction. It was Baine who was down. Caught in the role of his victims, he had done no better than they had.

Pace turned away, too numb for the sickness he knew he would soon feel. He had expected to die and almost

113

wished he had died. This would do Bim no good. It had changed things in the Bedrock, but that was of no use, either. He found himself moving toward the hotel where Bim lay, drawn helplessly, as spent as if his own life had run out.

Lafe Loving stood on the sidewalk at the foot of the filthy stairs. Pace had only to lift an inquiring eyebrow for Loving to answer his question.

"No change."

There was no point in climbing the stairs. Bim didn't want him up there, anyhow. Loving must know what had happened, but he left it to Pace to mention it. Arliss must have heard, too, and Pace wondered what difference it would make to her, now that he had blood on his hands. And the law to face. Detested as Baine had been among the decent element, he had died at the hands of another man.

He heard Loving's voice say, "You all right?"

"He burned me. That's all. Who's Alper's deputy here?"

"Ike Patterson. Good man. He won't want anymore from you than it takes to write Baine off."

Probably, but it didn't much matter. Pace walked on to the edge of town and kept going, following the path to the point above the town and river. There he slumped down wearily, his back against a boulder, sick now and fully spent. He had mated with death, the deepest of lusts, and found it wholly evil.

It was getting light when he came out of the stupor into which he had sunk. The town below was already stirring, the violence of the night put behind by the bustle of a newborn day. He pushed up, his knee painful and stiff, a hot streak burning above his belt. He descended to the town, hoping that by now he could go unnoticed. In main part he did, but now and then men gave him the sharp attention some of them might recently have bestowed on Baine. Ignoring these, Pace made his way to Bim's involuntarily chosen hotel.

When he saw a half dozen of his men gathered on the sidewalk, his heart sank. Then he realized that they, too, had been drawn there for the latest word.

They nodded their greetings, and Froggy Jorgensen said, "Doc Tryon just come down. He says Bim's turned the corner. There's a long haul yet, but his chances are better than even. I say that's good enough for Bimbo. He'll make it."

A feeling of gratitude such as Pace had never known welled up. It included these men. He wished he could

thank them for their concern and loyalty, but he was
without the words to do it. He turned and climbed the
stairs, bent on seeing Bim whether Bim wanted it or didn't.
Varley was in the room with the patient. He nodded,
understood, and went out. Pace sat down on the chair
Varley had vacated. Bim seemed asleep, but his color was
better, his body no longer unresting.

Pace sat without moving through a long moment. Then
he said quietly, "Bim? You hear me? I want you to just
listen. I know what's in your mind against me. There's
every reason for it to be there. Pretty soon you'll hear
about Baine, and I know how you'll see it. Your big
brother again. Saving you from bad men as well as from
bad girls. And from the bad mistakes you'd make if I let
you really fill your job on the ranch."

Bim turned his head. He had been awake but hadn't
wanted to acknowledge his brother. His eyes were clear
and bewildered. He had never expected anything like this
humble candor.

"I wanted Jinx Renner," Pace continued. "But I never
trifled with her. Everything that happened, she brought
about to bedevil me and split you and me farther apart.
What Baine said to you was an outright lie, but that's not
why I braced him. He was a coward. I hoped I could
break him down and make him show it to this town. That
would have been the end of him. But he wouldn't have
it that way. He drew on me."

"And you killed him." Bim nodded his head wearily.
"You could and you would. You're sure hell on wheels,
Pace Larabee. Take over and do it better than I can,
every time." He laughed harshly. "Even with Jinx. You
even had *her* coming to *you*."

"Easy, there. Don't know if the doc wants you to talk
yet."

"I'm talking. Any you listen. I'm not jealous of Jinx. I
only turned to her after Wendy turned against me, trying
to show her I didn't care. But I sure God objected to you
cutting in to see what you could get for yourself. It was
even an insult to Jinx, pegging her that low down. If you
got anywhere in her affections, you trifled with her, no
matter what you say about it."

"Her affections?" Pace gasped.

"She never bothered to hate a man before. Not the way
she hates you. Why you?"

"Not because I—"

Bim cut him off with a throaty laugh. Pace stared at
him helplessly, then got to his feet. Bim thought he had

115

lied about Jinx, had lied about not killing Baine because the man had nearly killed his kid brother.

"All I can say is I'm almighty sorry."

In the hallway he told Varley that he and Loving were to stay in town with Bim as long as needed. As soon as possible, Bim was to be moved to better quarters. He doubted that Bim would ever come back to the Bedrock. But as long as he could he intended to do the best he could for him. That was the pattern of his own life, as inescapable as his shadow. A man couldn't shake himself loose from the complexities and demands of his own nature. He knew that now. He would no longer fight it.

He found Ike Patterson in his office at the town jail. The fact that the deputy hadn't come looking for him promised a minimum of legal trouble. Patterson bore that out, although his expression was glum.

"The law's not going to be your problem, Larabee," he said. "Baine's record, and the fact that several men heard him threaten your life and seen him start a draw will settle that. What worries me, and had better worry you, is his friends in the badlands. Their breed don't take to having one of their kind beat by a decent citizen. It reflects on the reputation they all glory in and rely on. Hank Alper told me about the trouble you've had with them already. From here on, you better have eyes on all four sides of your head."

Pace said impatiently, "You going to need me for an inquest?"

Patterson shook his head. "I got some statements. I'll take yours. Then bury the whole thing as deep in the files as I can shove it."

CHAPTER 17

Pace stood with his feet braced on a high limb, his back to the trunk of a pine, and his spyglasses trained on the country below and eastward from him. It was the tree he had climbed once before to take a look at the outlaw camp. The camp was still there, but he could see no one in sight. He almost dared to hope that, with Baine dead his followers would disband and return to their former haunts.

It had been Baine who attracted and held them together. His elimination would at least have threatened Gilgen's hold on them, while weakening his influence with the nesters. Pace had been encouraged to think that this latter element had had second thoughts. He had been able to make his way this deep into the hills without being challenged. At least they weren't guarding the backway, as they were doing the last time he tried to penetrate the area. It could be they had decided he was a better neighbor than his enemies. Yet it wasn't all to the good. If his hold was slipping, Gilgen would have to move swiftly or find himself with little support beyond Howie Renner's. So far, in the week since the killing in Rowel, there had been no such move.

Shifting position, Pace turned the glasses toward Silver Butte. He could see the rotting headworks of the old mine, but the timber cut off Renner's house and outbuildings. Deciding to learn all he could while he was in the vicinity, he worked his way to the ground. Mounting, he headed west into an area still strange to him, that lying beyond the timber and on the butte's left flank.

He rode for some distance, cutting around the curve of the butte, before he bore in directly toward it. This, when he had climbed the backslope, would put him behind and above the Renner setup. But he had ridden only a short while before he came to a deeply cut creek, which drained that side of the butte and ran off to the west. He couldn't get across its trench at that point, so he turned downstream, riding quietly through the timber. And all at once

117

he stopped the horse, staring with keen interest into a short, widened stretch in the shallow canyon below him.

The creek pooled, down there, and someone was swimming in the still, crystalline water. He could see a head of long, pasted dark hair and the shimmering gleam of a body slithering lazily in the water. Clothing lay on the sandy flat beyond, and a pair of small boots. There was no horse, so the spot must be within walking distance of the old mine. The submerged, opaque shape riveted his eyes. It moved languorously as she swam to shallow water.

When he realized that she was coming out, he swung back from sight. The horse seemed as reluctant as he to leave the spot, and that was no way for either of them to feel about Jinx Renner. He rode on aimlessly, about decided to forget Silver Butte and go back down to the basin. Each step of the horse increased the foment in him. He bore it helplessly, knowing that it would never leave him until it was exorcised. There was only one way to do that. He swung the horse and rode back to his previous point of vantage.

He slid out of the saddle, his heart hammering, and trailed reins. There were several places where he could descend without the horse. He chose one and started, working his way quietly and carefully. This brought him down to creek level below the pool. His knees were weak, his cheeks hot, his mind focused. He came to the lower end of the pool and stopped.

He didn't know whether he was relieved or disappointed that she had dressed. Her feet and legs were still bare, but she had put on a skirt and blouse and was combing her wet hair. There was a somber, reflective look to her he had never seen there before. She still thought she was alone. This, he realized, was the only time he had seen her in repose, her guard down, her bright, saucy manner gone. Unfortunately, he liked the change although it didn't lessen his resentment of what she had done to him and, through him, to Bim.

And then she looked up, turned her head and saw him. She made no sound, standing transfixed, a stricken look twisting her features. But she didn't move when he started on toward her.

"What's the trouble, hellcat?" he taunted. "Wondering how long I've been here?"

"Leave—me be," she said weakly.

"Sure." He stopped in front, boldly inspecting her from tip to toe. "You can have your little games, no matter who gets hurt in them. But don't hurt Jinx just because she

118

likes her peculiar brand of fun. Oh, no. When it comes to Jinx, king's ex."

She lifted her head. Her voice was steadier. "If you're talking about what happened to Bim, I had nothing to do with it."

"Except to set him up for Baine's gun."

She sighed. "I knew you'd think that. But I didn't."

"Only you and me knew what's passed between us," he said relentlessly. "So how did Baine know how to goad Bim into pulling on him? And how come you got Bim fighting mad, that same night?"

She made a gesture of despair with her hands. "It just happened that way. Stella knew how I'd been teasing you. Women tell each other things like that. I had no idea she'd blab to Howie and how they'd use it." She lifted pleading eyes. "Go away? I won't ever bother you again."

"I aim to make sure."

He caught and pulled her to him. She didn't fight back or scream and this passivity only goaded him on. Her failure to scream confirmed his guess that they were out of earshot of the Renner house. Her failure to fight puzzled, but did not deter him. He lifted, carried her onto the deeper sand, and put her down. The fight was gone, even though he worked his will on her. And then he saw the tears that leaked from under her closed eyes.

He rose to his feet, drunkenly dizzy. She didn't open her eyes. Turning, he slipped away, walking swiftly over the soft sand. When he reached the rim and looked down, she still lay there. He hurried on to his horse.

Unwilling to assume that the empty outlaw camp meant anything hopeful, Pace rounded out the day by inspecting the summer range, finding nothing to disturb him. The men now camped there had nothing to report, and it could have been any other summer season.

In late afternoon he rode down to the lower basin. The haying was well under way and moving without a hitch. He went on to headquarters, dreading the end of the action afforded by the day's demands. He was afraid of the thoughts he had repressed since leaving that lonely little swimming place. They wouldn't be the gratified thoughts of a man who, at last, had conquered a woman.

He had reached the day corral before he came out of his thoughts. The horse Arliss kept in town for her occasional use was there. He had hardly thought of the promise she had made since the night she made it, supposing that his meeting Baine, after all, had canceled it. She had never come there unless Bim was at headquarters, making them a proper threesome in the big house. His first thought was of what the men would think about it, with Bim not there. They all knew what Baine had said to Bim, and their imaginations had had a week to work on it.

He didn't hurry taking care of his horse. And it took a mental squaring of the shoulders when he crossed the compound to the house. Arliss was in the living room, busy with her embroidery. One look told him that she, too, was nervous.

She said, with an unconvincing lightness, "Well, here I am."

He nodded, wondering if she meant that she was there as promised. "I take it Bim's doing all right."

"He's coming along fine. They moved him to a much better hotel, thank heaven. The doctor said he'll be as good as new in a few more weeks."

Pace studied her masked face, trying to add it up. Baine hadn't killed him, after all, Bim was better, and that seemed to have put them back where they were the night she promised herself to him. But he didn't want her. Slim, nubile, attractive though she still was, he just didn't want her. Yet he didn't know how to tell her so when he couldn't tell her why. He didn't really know why, himself, for she was the same woman he had yearned for so long.

He had no doubt of what was on her mind when she took it for granted that this was a special occasion. Often she ate at the cookshack, too, when she was on the ranch. Now she took over the big house kitchen. He washed up on the back porch and heard her busy in there, making sounds that should have been cheering and rewarding to him. He wondered if it would be better to shake the nagging doubts from his mind and let this night seal their future.

When they had eaten supper, and he was drawing on a flat-tasting cigar, Arliss said, "I want to stay here, Pace, and never go back to Rowel."

He managed to keep from frowning. "How about your business?"

"I've had a standing offer for it for quite a while. I'm going to take it. And there's another thing, while we're on the subject. You're a going concern now. It wouldn't be like it was the first time you tried to borrow money. Any bank would be glad to accommodate you. I want you to do it and buy my share of the ranch, just as soon as you can arrange it."

He leaned forward, amazed and for some reason wary. "Why?"

"Bim should be your partner, not me. I want you to take him in." She smiled. "I'll be happy in a woman's place, here on your ranch."

"Bim doesn't want it. I doubt that he'll ever be back here."

Arliss shook her head. "He loved the Bedrock. I think he'd come back if you'd treat him as an equal. I want you to do what I ask. Will you?"

It seemed a generous thought, well intended. Yet, something bothered him. He had a feeling that, once again, she was revealing only as much of herself and her mind as she had to in order to persuade him.

He said, "What will you do with the money? Try to buy off Tex Gilgen?" The way she lifted her head and masked her eyes convinced him. "No smoke, Arliss. Not unless, for once, you dig all the way to the bottom."

"Oh, Pace. I came out here to be nice to you. And you're trying to quarrel."

"Why do you need the money?"

"Won't you just—?"

"No, I won't just," he cut in. "I don't want a woman who'll show me the least of herself she can. Show me all of it, or you'll have to sell your interest in this concern to somebody else."

She looked away for a long moment. That didn't completely hide the desperation in her eyes. Sure she would keep her promise, if he humored her. But keeping it wasn't the real reason she had come out here.

"All right, Pace." Her voice was despairing. "I hoped to keep your good opinion, but you won't let it be that way. I'm in awful trouble. I have been ever since Tex found me here. You see—" She hesitated, then rushed on. "I wasn't the one who cleaned up in the mining venture in Blackhawk. It was Tex. I took the money and ran away from him."

"Stole it?"

"He calls it that. So would you. So, I guess, would the law."

"Can a wife steal from her husband?"

She swallowed, then said helplessly, "I wasn't his wife. I—I was his mistress."

He could only look at her, dumbfounded.

"Don't blame me too much," she said miserably. "I was young and hungry and inexperienced. He's proved, out here, what kind of man he was. While I've grown up and

121

found a new life and—and met the man I really want."

"I see. He's been stopped from taking over the ranch to get back his money. So he's demanding outright restitution. That or he'll send you over the road."

She nodded her head. "He doesn't think he's been stopped. But it's turned out to be a tougher nut than he thought he had to crack. He counted on Baine's help, but he can get along without it, and he told me to tell you that. But that it would be easier all around if I just returned the money, and he called off the war and left the country."

"He want you back with the money?"

"He did till I convinced him my feeling for him is dead."

"The night he socked you."

She colored and nodded her head.

"Well, you've told me. Now you can tell him I said he can go straight to hell."

Her mouth dropped open. "Pace! Why?"

"I'm not buying a dishonest woman from him to live with on a ranch built with dishonest money. I agree you found the man you want, but you don't want him the way he wanted you. You could have married me at any time, Arliss. You still don't want to. But now you're got to have my protection, in return for which you'll pay in a woman's coin." He grimaced. "As long as you need protection."

She looked at him in disbelief, then her expression changed. Her mouth twisted, and her eyes hardened. "I see. The gossip's true. You've been carrying on with that hussy, Jinx Renner. The toy of every randy saddlebum in the hills."

He was startled to hear himself say heatedly, "I haven't been carrying on with her. But she's no hussy and she's no toy."

"You fool. But all right. I'll go back to town."

He nodded. "It'll be dark before you can get there. I'll send a man in with you."

"Don't bother." Her smile was anything but pretty. "I can take care of myself. I always have. I always will."

"I truly hope you can make good on that."

He rose from the table and for a moment watched her, wondering what she would do now that the refuge she had counted on had been denied her. He had no doubt that she would find something. In the other critical turns of her life she seemed to have done very well. She looked back with an indifference that not long ago would have dismayed him. He knew then that a man had only one meaning to her, his usefulness to her. And his was gone.

122

He found Calhoun and told him to saddle her horse. The old man looked at him with wise eyes, then shuffled off to the corral. Going on down to the creek, Pace waited there, drawing on the bitter cigar. Then Arliss came out of the house, mounted the horse Cal had ready, and rode off down the trail to town.

That was easier to face than what she had left behind. The fact that the Bedrock had been founded on dishonest money. In reality, Tex Gilgen had been his backer and partner and still was. Yet Pace wouldn't have changed what he had told Arliss to tell the man. Gilgen had chosen the method of settling accounts, himself.

CHAPTER 18

The voice from the doorway had only to penetrate a light and unresting sleep. "Pace? Spud Stevens is downstairs and says he's gotta talk to you."

Instantly awake, Pace sat up in bed. Swede O'Brien stepped into the dark room. "He's got his girl along," the puncher went on. "Banged the bunkhouse door, not knowing where to find you. All he'd say was he had to see you."

Pace was already dressing, a feeling rising that this was the end of the waiting he had endured through the several days since he sent his reply to Gilgen through Arliss.

"Tell him I'll be right down."

O'Brien turned and left.

It would take something important to bring Stevens out of the hills in the dead of night to see a man he hated implacably. Pace stepped onto the balcony in time to see the puncher light a lamp in the room below him. He was down there himself when O'Brien brought in the visitors. One look showed Pace they were both charged with tension.

Pace nodded, guarded until he knew what it was about. "Howdy, Spud, and you, too, Wendy. Have seats."

"No time to set." Stevens' voice was hard and clipped. "I want you to send my girl to town."

"At this late date?" Pace stared at him. "How come?"

"All hell's busting loose," Stevens said in a rushing voice. "Now Gilgen claims he owns Bedrock Ranch. Says it was built on money stole from him, and he's taking it over lock, stock and barrel. Says that was always the case. That he didn't feel like explaining till now, because of some woman's reputation. That wolf pack Baine brought down from the back country had started to drift off. Now they're gathering around Gilgen, smelling blood and pickings again. Me, I've had enough of that bunch for neighbors." Stevens looked at Pace, all but glaring. "I'd rather put up with you."

"Thanks." Another time, Pace would have marveled at such a change. There was too much pressure for it now. "How does Gilgen figure to do this taking over?" he asked.

124

"By running off you and your men. Or beefing the lot of you if you don't run. Me, I reckon you'll run."

"When's it set for?"

"Tonight—tomorrow night." Stevens shrugged. "I ain't sure, but it'll be one or the other. I just learned today. But I had to wait till night to make sure I got Wendy out of the basin."

"Why didn't you take her to town, yourself?" Pace asked. "You're gonna need all the help you can get."

Their glances held for a moment. In spite of the urgency, Pace felt something warm flood him. Here was a proud, stubborn man whose convictions had been changed in spite of himself and who was man enough to act accordingly.

Pace looked at Wendy. "Agree with your dad?" She nodded somberly. "I'll send you in with Cal Calhoun. He'll get you there. A couple of my men are there, and they'll take care of you. I hope you'll help them take care of Bim."

"I'd like to take care of him all the time," she replied softly. "It's my fault he nearly got himself killed. I told him, once, that he didn't have any backbone. I keep thinking that's why he braced Baine."

Pace knew that wasn't the reason except in the sense that all things bore on all things else. But Bim needed this contrite, warm and lovely girl. So let her feel herself to blame until time and young blood got them straightened out.

Pace hurried out to the yard. The bunkhouse was lighted and astir, with some of the men in the yard. O'Brien had gathered enough to know a crisis was at hand without understanding its particulars. Pace relayed the information the nester had given him. He didn't like the change he saw in the men, although he didn't blame them for it. They had been required to hold themselves in beyond enduring. At last the enemy was bringing the fight to them, and they rose to it, welcomed it, were ready.

He had Cal saddle horses and watched him leave for Rowel with Wendy. The look on the hill girl's face told him her sole purpose, now, was to go to Bim, to make him well again, to make things right between them.

It was Stevens' opinion that attacks would be launched simultaneously on headquarters and the outcamp in the hills. Pace decided at once to pull the men in from the camp, if there was time. The raiders wouldn't bother the cattle until they had dealt with the men defending the ranch. He sent word to the summer range and detailed

125

other men to stand sentry duty on the approaches to head-quarters.

The night wore on and then away without further developments. The longer he waited the more restive Pace became. He had gained enough in self-understanding to realize his loner instinct was behind his mood. He had founded the Bedrock, and it still seemed to him that it was his place to protect it. The way to do that was to remove Gilgen and Renner from the equation, as Baine had been removed. He kept hunting a way to do it and save the basin from the blood bath he had stood off at such pains for so long.

The men came in from the summer range shortly after daylight. They, too, had caught the fever of the men already at headquarters. They all took turns eating breakfast, most of them too high-keyed to do more than nibble a little food and drink coffee. When he had eaten his own morning meal, Pace told them casually that he was going to do some poking around. They were used to this habit and asked no questions. It was unlikely that any move would be launched against the ranch during daylight hours, but he reminded them not to bank on that. Then he saddled a horse and struck off for the hills, determined to play out his own string before another night arrived.

An hour later he was at Pistol Peak where, with the killing of Cob Durnbo, it had all begun. How long ago that seemed, how much had changed since then, and yet how little had been settled. Sheltered in the broken outskirts of the pinnacle, itself, he rested his horse and smoked a cigarette. Cobble Gap lay ahead and below him, and he pondered whether to check the outlaw camp or ride the backway to Silver Butte. The latter was his ultimate goal. But it would be well to know where the outlaws that Gilgen had remustered were keeping themselves.

By the time he had finished his smoke, he had decided to give himself every advantage he could. He entered the gap boldly. The Stevens hound pack was still up there, but its warning would serve him as well as his enemies. But he reached the fork without hearing a sound from them. This puzzled him, for at this point they had usually picked him up, even when they were being kept in the Stevens pocket. He rode on up Cobble, splashing through the water, not relaxing his vigilance in spite of the quietness.

He came onto the bench by way of the cleft and topped out in a scene of tranquillity. The area was deserted, restored to its pristine loneliness. He crossed the flat to where the camp had been. Nothing remained of it but litter.

Baine's day was over, and so were whatever schemes he had had in his crafty head. Pace rode on, curious about the Stevens pocket. There was a well-worn trail to follow down from there. He moved slowly, expecting at any moment to be picked up by the dogs. He aroused no response from them, even when he followed a steep, twisting trail down into the pocket.

Either the dogs had been removed purposely or Stevens, knowing he wouldn't be able to care for them, had turned them loose to fend for themselves. If this were the case, they might already have struck off into the deeper hills on a hunt for food. He hoped this was the explanation. If they had been taken to Silver Butte for sentry duty, it meant Renner's place had been turned into an armed camp, and he would never even get near it.

He rode in to the sorry set of buildings that had been Wendy's home for so long, struck anew by the loyalty that had kept her divided heart fixed to her hard-bitten father. He hoped she would give Bim reason to stay in the Bedrock. But her loyalty would now attach to Bim, as it had to Spud, and she would go where Bim went. For Pace had no doubt that they would make their peace, and she would never come back to this lonely setting. If Bim stayed, healed of his wound and his bitterness—but many uncertainties had to be resolved before that could even be considered.

He rode down Sand Creek until he found a way to climb onto the western benchland. Early sun by then splashed over the high country, throwing the shadows of the hills over the plateau below them. As always happened when he was alone with nature, he began to respond to its wild order, its controlled savagery, its demand that all its creatures prove themselves. This wrought in him an unexpected feeling of kinship with Stevens. And at least a sympathy for all the nester kind, which took so naturally to a place like this. It struck him that he had made his peace with them, too. He wondered how many of them, like Stevens, had come to regard him as a better neighbor than the ones they had befriended and helped so long.

He headed toward Silver Butte along the route that had brought him upon Jinx in her private swimming hole. If he wasn't betrayed by sentry dogs, this would give him a look at the area before he made his final move. He came to the fateful little creek and found the beat of his heart affected. He would rather not have revisited her canyon-locked retreat, but he had an idea that the course she took using it would be a good one for him to follow. He left the horse where he had before, took his rifle from the boot and slung the strap of his field glasses over his shoulder.

Descended to the creek, he stopped for a moment on the tiny sand flat that betrayed no hint, now, of its secrets. Moving on, he found that a well-worn trail followed the stream upward. Jinx had come there often, and it struck him again how little he had known of her and her mostly solitary life. He followed her path, moving with extreme care, his ears acutely keening for the dreaded baying of hounds.

After about a quarter of a mile, the trail left the bottom and climbed out. Pace went up in slow steps, for the bright sun above meant that there was no concealing timber up there. He came out into a rocky waste, the butte rising hard to the left. He had circled it to its back side, still without raising an alarm. Resting, he formed a mental picture of the old mine, which he had always approached from the far side. If he went on around the shoulder of the butte, he would be south of Renner's house. And his scent must already be close enough to be picked up by the dogs, if they were being used here now.

Encouraged to think that Stevens had given them their freedom before he quit the hills, Pace moved on. But he had barely crossed the rough ground when he hauled up short, staring hard. He was atop a low cliff and below him spread a scene he was more familiar with. Far down was the notch dropping to Sand Creek where Howie Renner had tried to dry-gulch him. Closer, on the left, was the woods into which he had taken Jinx, that same night. The southern exposure of the Renner house and outbuildings was nearer, and on his left. Yet what most riveted his attention was the answer to what had happened to Baine's old camp.

Off to the right, but within shouting range of the house, was a new and equally large camp. Pace put his glasses on it, although without them he could see men in numbers moving about. The sharper study let him estimate them at close to a dozen. There were picketed horses at least equalling that number on beyond the camp. The activity at the moment was that of men idling while remaining alerted and on call.

He shifted the glasses until they were fixed on the Renner place, itself. No one was in sight there, but smoke drifted lazily from the chimney of the house. Someone was cooking or had just cooked the morning meal. He wondered if this had been Jinx or pneumatic, drunken Stella. Of greater concern was the immediate whereabouts

128

of Howie and Gilgen, who would certainly be on hand at a time like this.

Casing the glasses, Pace picked up his rifle and moved to the left in careful steps. He could have gotten down at any point but he stayed on the rim top until he was immediately above the abandoned mine. There he descended and quickly concealed himself in the brush that had overgrown the surface of the old workings. This put him close enough to keep tabs and yet left him room to maneuver.

The spot was hot, for the mounting sun beat directly on it and the brush offered poor shade. It seemed a long while before Gilgen and Howie came out of the house together, descending the high front steps and striking off toward the new camp. Pace let them get well away from there before he began to move, working his way carefully to the rear of the house.

He went in through the kitchen doorway, and there was Jinx, sitting at an uncleared breakfast table drinking coffee. Her thoughts seemed far away but, as if drawn by instinct, her eyes moved and settled on him. They widened, but she said nothing at all.

He said quietly, "Where's Stella?"

She hesitated, then said in a rather loud voice, "In bed. Drunk. Where else?"

"Take me there. Ahead of me. And don't try anything."

Her lip curled. "You got your randy mind fixed on her, this time?"

"Keep quiet."

Jinx rose from the table, scorn and defiance on her face in spite of her obedience. She was back in shirt and Levi's, but his head swam with memories. He hated to do this to her, but he had no choice. Stella's bedroom proved to be behind a curtain off the adjoining room. The woman lay there in sodden sleep, as Jinx had said. He looked at Jinx. She responded with a stony stare, but her cheeks were flushed, not drained.

Pace's plan had included Stella, too. Clearly, she would be more burden than help to him. He looked back at Jinx and caught a thoughtful frown on her face.

"Come over, Jinx," he said quietly. "You know what's planned. It's got to be stopped. You could help me do it."

"Me go over to your side?" She snorted. "Not in a million years."

She turned with a toss of the head and went back to the kitchen. Pace followed, his spirit unaccountably burdened. Where once she might have been won away from this kind of life, he had put her back solidly on the side of her

129

people. The other Jinx, the girl who had emerged briefly on the last few of their encounters, was gone. Returned was the hard, brassy vixen of the back country. Abruptly, saving that shy, uncertain, womanly other-girl was more important to him than saving Bedrock Ranch.

Stella's ears were probably as insensate as her other faculties, but he spoke in a lowered voice. "I've got to tell you this. I'm sorry for a lot of things. For the way I misjudged the nesters. The way I fouled up Bim. But most of all, I'm sorry for the way I treated you, the way I pegged you, the way I wouldn't let myself admit the truth. Which is that you and I don't belong on opposite sides and never did."

She stamped an impatient foot. "Whatever you come here for, get on with it! Will you?"

He sighed, convinced that he had put her forever beyond the reach of any words of his. Yet, knowing that each minute he tarried there increased the danger to him, he had to persist.

"I'm getting on with what matters most to me, Jinx. You. I love you. I'd have known it at the start if I hadn't been what you called me the night we danced together in Rowel. A bigheaded, pigheaded would-be cattle king. Remember?"

Her cheeks colored, and she turned her head quickly, unwilling for him to look into her eyes. "What do you expect all this to get you?" she asked.

"At least a friend in place of an enemy. I'm tired of being a loner, Jinx, and so are you. For you've been one. You've had to be, not belonging to the world you had to live in and making yourself think you despised the other world because you thought it despised you."

"Because I thought it did?" She swung toward him, anger flashing in her wonderful eyes. "Did anybody ever work harder at proving it than you did, Pace Larabee? It's a little late for you to come around saying that, all the while, you loved me. And it's a mite too feeble to cozy me out of the help you want from me, whatever it is."

"I only wanted to win your help," Pace said with a sigh. "If that's impossible, I've got to take it, because time won't wait. Write a note to leave for Gilgen and Howie. Tell them I've got you and you'll be at my headquarters, which they better remember before they attack. Say the only way they'll get you back is to come there, just the two of them, for a talk with me. I've got a deal that might interest Gilgen, at least."

"You think they'd deal with you," she said scornfully, "after the way you—abused me, the other day?"

"That's not what's pushing them. I don't think you even told them about it." Her cheeks colored, and he knew she had not. "Come on. I'm in a hurry."

A thick voice said behind him, "Huh-uh, Larabee. You ain't in no hurry."

CHAPTER 19

Pace whirled to see Stella standing framed by the inside doorway. She held a handgun, and her body wove, but she was in no helpless drunken condition. Jinx had known this all along. She had tricked him and warned Stella of what was taking place, then had stalled along until Stella took over. When he looked back at her, Jinx confirmed this with a contemptuous smile.

"You sure took your time, Stella," she snapped.

"It was so nice listening to them pretty things he said," Stella answered. "I hated to break it up."

Jinx scowled. "Pull his fangs."

Stella reached to take his rifle. Pace knew from her mean, bloodshot eyes that she would shoot him without compunction. He let her have the rifle and balanced to make a grab for her when she tried to empty his holster. But Stella was too wily for that. She stepped back out of reach and nodded to Jinx, her six-gun never leaving him. Jinx took the pistol and also stepped back quickly.

"Want me to go get the boys?" Stella asked.

Somewhat to Pace's surprise, Jinx shook her head. "They'd kill him, and I don't want him dead—not yet. We'll stash him in the old mine, Stella, and he'll be our secret. Yours and mine. Understand?"

"Yours and my secret?" Stella asked eagerly. "Or yours and my man?"

Jinx cut her a look of annoyance. "Get your mind back on your bottle, Stella. I'll handle this end of it."

Stella sighed, turned and disappeared. Jinx still held his pistol, and Pace doubted that she would quail, another time, at using it. Her hatred of him had been driven in deep.

"Get walking," she snapped.

His shoulders slumped, Pace walked out through the doorway and across the back porch. He heard the thump of her boot heels on the boards as he went down the steps. All her spunk and hurt and resentment were in the sounds. His searching eyes showed him no place ahead where he might stand a chance to turn the tables. Even if she couldn't bring herself to gun him down, a shot into the air would bring a nest of hornets swarming over him. He plodded on through the brush, climbing the grade.

He came to the mine adit, stopped and turned. She glared at him, and it was hard to remember that, only days ago, he had conquered and bent her to his will.

"I meant every word I said back there," he told her quietly. "When nature turned out a pair like us, it was for better than trying to destroy each other. Take the gun off me, Jinx. Help me talk sense into Gilgen and Howie."

Her mouth opened. For a breath he thought he had moved her his way a little. Then scorn came back into her eyes, and she tossed her dark head. "How you keep talking your pretty talk. Hush it and get yourself in that mine."

Pace turned and walked through the shadow into the opening of the mine. He saw how she could hold him there. Just within the portal was an ancient plank wall with a heavy door. The main shaft of the old silver workings would have been vertical, so this would have been a drift cut for ventilation or drainage. He had to stoop to go through the doorway. The interior was empty save for dust, cobwebs, mustiness and litter from some bygone time. He expected Jinx to say something more, but the next thing he knew she had slammed the door shut behind him.

He looked around. Because of cracks between the planks of the wall, the light wasn't cut off completely. He heard the rasp of metal and knew she was securing the door from the outside.

"You hear me?" she called through the cracks. "If you go poking back into the mine without a light, you'll wind up at the bottom of a shaft."

"Damn it, Jinx, listen—!"

He heard her laugh trail off as she left.

He gave her time to get well away before he began an inspection of the heavy barricade shutting him in. It left him disconsolate. He sat hunkered on his heels, rubbing his jaw with dusty fingers. In the end it had been little Jinx who brought down the giant of the Bedrock. He didn't feel like a giant. On the other hand he didn't feel like something that belonged in a cave.

He didn't figure on staying there, either. Yet he didn't discount her warning about trying to escape through some other surface opening of the mine. He walked back into the tunnel until he could no longer see at all, feeling out each step with his feet, hoping to locate something with which he could batter, pry or tear his way out of there. He found nothing. Not unmindful of the danger of mine gas, he struck a match. The flickering light showed him no tool. But the timbering was split and spintery from long years of drying out. He managed to pull off a large sliver. He used another match to get this lighted, making a brand that would burn longer.

The tunnel floor was unbroken as far ahead as he could see. He went on, his mind shut to the danger of an explosion or a cave-in behind him. He stopped presently to find another flare and light it from the used-up one. The cramped, stuffy space was already hot and smoky. Something scurried past him, a rat. He knew he should turn back, but he couldn't bring himself to give up.

He had lighted yet another firebrand, and knew he had moved a perilous distance into the smelly bowels of the earth, when he found what he wanted. It wasn't much of a tool, a spiked candlestick that some long-gone miner had driven into a timber. It was rusty but sound, and he had trouble pulling it out.

On his way back to the tunnel mouth he picked up a large chunk of quartz waste. He could see only a pinpoint of light ahead when the brand he carried gave out. He dropped it, ground out the embers and scraped dust over it with his foot. Then he moved on without much hope that he had helped himself. The better light and fresher air behind the barricade were achievements enough momentarily. There he rested to cool off and catch his breath. Then he went to work.

The shrinkage that had opened the cracks in the wooden wall had also altered the fit of the door. Moving purposely, now, he quickly located the strap-iron hasp, outside, with which Jinx had secured the door after she slammed it shut. The lack of bolt heads or nuts on his side indicated that the hasp was latched over a heavy staple. He worked the spike end of the candlestick through the crack until it came against the strap. Then he delivered a whacking blow with the quartz he held in the other hand.

Metal snapped against metal, but that was all that happened.

He struck again and another three or four times before something gave enough for him to be sure it had done so. He stopped to scrub sweat and dust from his face with his sleeve. Then he struck his end of the crude tool so hard the quartz shattered. But he was hardly conscious of that, for there was a clanging rattle and the spike sank deep into the crack. Then there was only the wedge it made, to hold the door shut. The stapled end of the hasp had been torn free. He worked the tool until he could pull it free, and then he pushed the door outward.

He went out into air and sunshine that, by contrast, was cool and dazzling. He stood there catching his breath and letting his eyes adjust to the light. Then he shut the door, set the loosened staple back into place and tapped it in with a rock. From the outside there was nothing to show that the prisoner wasn't still within. Then he started down toward the house.

He came up to it with even greater caution than he had exercised before. Stopped as close to the back door as he dared go, he listened intently for a moment without hearing a sound from inside. He moved quietly across the porch to see through the door that the kitchen was empty. He also saw how sure Jinx had been that she had put him out of action. His pistol still lay on the table, and his rifle leaned against a wall. But at that moment Stella came weaving through the inner doorway. She looked straight at him.

"Man," she said in her whiskey voice, "it's no wonder Jinx went *loco* over you. How in hell did you get out of that gopher hole?"

Her darting eyes belied her lazy manner. She made a lurching dart toward the table and the handgun that lay there. She was only a step short when Pace collided and sent her reeling. He picked up the gun with hasty fingers. She steadied herself and glared at him. He edged over and got hold of his rifle. He studied her hard eyes and ruined face. The fact that she had made no outcry informed him that she had no allies nearby.

"I'm putting *you* in that mine, Stella," he threatened. "Then I'm heading for the ranch. It's hot and dry and smelly in there. It might be a long time before anybody figures out what become of you. You'll miss your bottle."

"No." She was aghast. "Don't do that."

"Rather talk a little?" he asked.

She was instantly hostile again, but his threat of depriving her of her booze had really scared her. "Talk about what?" she asked hesitantly.

"Where did Jinx go and why?"

Stella frowned, afraid to answer truthfully, afraid not to. "She don't butt in on my business. I don't butt in on hers."

"All right. Get walking."

Stella tossed her head, then the fight ran out of her and her shoulders slumped. "All right. She went over to the camp to see Howie and Tex. I don't know what for."

135

Pace frowned. "I thought she wasn't ready to have me killed yet."

"You're the one trying to get yourself killed, you mule-head," Stella retorted. "She only put you in that mine to keep you from it. She never said as much, but I'm a woman. I know the signs."

"Signs of what?"

"Ain't you the modest one. You think she'd let them wolves tear you to pieces, the one man around who could tame her? Believe you me, they'd tear you to pieces if they got their hands on you. They ain't forgot Les Baine. And poking around like you do, they'd sure God of nailed you."

There was a strong likelihood of that, even yet, but he couldn't share her view of Jinx's feelings and motives.

"You're courting a long dry spell," he told her regretfully. "Unless you feel like loosening your tongue more than that."

She sighed. "What else you want to know?"

"Why did Howie and Gilgen hustle over to the outlaw camp, a while ago?"

She licked her lips as though they were already parched. "They just found out Spud Stevens flew the coop last night and went over to your side. They figured on surprising you. Now they got to figure a new way."

The temperature seemed to have taken a fifty-degree drop. The obvious way to catch the Bedrock off guard, now, would be to hit it immediately, instead of waiting for night. Jinx's reason for trying to put him out of action hadn't been what Stella said, at all. She hadn't wanted him to gather the meaning of the activity that must be going on and get back to the ranch with it.

Forgetting Stella, he wheeled and plunged out of the house. His time sense was mixed up, but the sun told him it was midmorning. He had to move carefully in spite of his need to reach his horse and get back to headquarters. When he had climbed high enough on the butte, he took time to stop and look around. He still had the field glasses, but he didn't need them to see, to his dismay, that the outlaw camp was already empty. The horses that had been picketed there were gone. While he bumbled around in his chronic lonehandedness, doom had descended on the Bedrock.

He went plunging on along the twisting trail over the butte and down to Jinx's swimming hole. The quiet spot on the canyon-locked creek was again a reminder of his many stupidities. He crossed the canyon and climbed onto the far bench before he felt far enough away to move openly. He rushed on under the trees until he reached the place where he had left his horse.

It wasn't there.

It hadn't strayed off, for it was well trained and would have remained where it had been ground-tied. Puzzled, Pace searched the soft litter until he found a light impression of a hoof. It was south of where the animal had been left, and it pointed in the same southerly direction. He went on to a patch of open ground to pick up easily not one but two sets of horse tracks. Somebody had stumbled onto the horse, its brand betraying where it had come from. He went on to where the rim broke down to a small, natural ford in the creek. His horse was still being led at a steady gait, back toward the Renner setup.

And then he heard the beat of hoofs coming from behind him.

He crossed the creek, scrambled up the opposite bank and in behind a rock where he could watch and command the ford. It was only a moment later when two horsemen whipped up on the far side, and his breath checked. They filed out for the descent, and the lead rider was Tex Gilgen. Howie Renner came down behind him, and there were only the two of them. They were still in the water when Pace's shout ripped out.

"Hold up! Right there!"

They were caught flatfooted and knew it as they halted and looked upward, not knowing exactly where he was. He rose to his feet, the rifle lined on them. Howie stared up at him in openmouthed dismay. Gilgen's face darkened in a glower. They were both careful to keep their hands motionless and in sight. Les Baine's fate seemed to have given them respect for his marksmanship.

Pace studied them. Gilgen's eyes rubbed out the small hope that had brought him to Silver Butte. The eyes were full of hatred. What Gilgen saw was not only a man who had built a huge, prosperous ranch on ill-gotten money; he was also staring at the man he believed to have replaced him in the affections and the favors of a woman.

"Where's your wolf pack, Gilgen?" Pace asked. "Did you send them down to do your dirty work, while you and Howie play it safe up here?"

Gilgen made an angry toss of the head. "When I deal with you, bucko," he returned, "it'll be in person."

Pace hesitated. That sounded like the attack hadn't yet been launched, for some reason. He said in a less raking voice, "Then we can get on with what I come up here

137

about. I agree I owe you money, Gilgen, though I didn't know that till the other day. I'm making you a fair offer. I hope you've got sense enough left to take it."

Gilgen said suspiciously, "What's your offer?"

"I'll raise the money to pay you off. Direct and not through anyone else like you suggested a while back. You name a place, one a good long ways from here. The money'll be waiting there at Wells Fargo just as soon as you can get there. Providing, Gilgen, you agree to call it quits and never come back to this country."

Gilgen's eyes showed deep surprise. The effect on Howie was something else. He was slower to comprehend, but when he did his face twisted in distrust. He looked at Gilgen.

"Now, look here. You ain't skipping out with the profits after the help I been giving you. Not when it only takes a little push to pocket the whole caboodle."

"Let down your hackles," Gilgen snapped. "He already passed up the chance to square his debts with money." He cut his eyes to Pace again. "That's your answer, Larabee. What you gonna do about it, shoot me out of this saddle? I wouldn't recommend it. I got men all around here, beating the bushes for you. One shot, and they'll have you."

Showing a coolness Pace had never credited him with, Gilgen started his horse forward to climb out of the ford. Howie looked toward him helplessly, lacking the same kind of nerve by a considerable margin. Pace's fingers froze on the trigger of his rifle. He had no doubt that Gilgen's men were, as he had said, all around them. He couldn't take on all of them, and there was little hope of escape without a horse. His only chance lay in not advertising his location more widely. Instead of shooting, he cut back hastily into the brushy rock.

138

CHAPTER 20

For the moment, Pace judged, the three of them were on about an even footing. That was all Gilgen, himself, had hoped to gain from his icy-nerved gamble. Howie, who for bleak seconds had found himself alone, deserted, and under the gun of a man with every reason to hate him, would be in no rush to expose himself to that gun again. He would follow Gilgen's lead, now, and Gilgen's failure to fire a shot to bring help from the outlaws was encouraging to Pace. Gilgen had vowed to deal with him personally. His self-esteem prohibited his increasing the two-to-one advantage he already held over his enemy.

Pace weighed this even as he moved on an instinctive course of action. They would stalk him. They, too, would have to worry, for, cornered and desperate, he might lie doggo to settle with them individually before being overcome himself. His hope now was to outwit them in a game of cat-and-mouse, reducing if not removing his own handicap.

By the time Howie's horse had crashed up out of the ford behind Gilgen's, Pace had dropped off the cutbank and back into the canyon. He wanted distance between himself and them and hoped to gain it by doubling back. Yet he didn't try to avoid leaving sign. They would eventually pick it up, at best. If he was lucky, it might tow them into the lower country where he would have only the two of them to worry about.

He followed the creek bed a short distance before climbing out on the west bank. It was a sharp climb, and when he topped out he stopped for a moment to rest. Only because of this did he hear the sound with which he had grown so familiar—that of dogs far in the vague distance. He listened keenly, puzzled and worried. Whether or not they were running free, as he had earlier supposed, the hounds were a restored danger to him. They seemed to be somewhere off to the north, in the direction he had to move to get out of the high country.

Catching up his rifle, he moved on stubbornly, maintaining direction by keeping the high sun on his shoulders. In only a few moments he could no longer hear the hounds. Ten minutes later he had forgotten them for he had reached the south slope of Silver Butte and its more familiar landmarks. Far down the country he could see Pistol Peak, that earmark of his home range. He stopped again to rest, satisfied. The course he had followed suggested that he was fleeing toward the Bedrock summer camp and help, as fast as his feet could carry him. His pursuers wouldn't be so careful of their ownselves from here on.

Presently he went on, hunting the place for a stand. He was halfway down to Pistol Peak before he found it, an elevated point where he could watch the back trail without being exposed himself, and where the sound of gunfire could scarcely carry as far as Silver Butte. It gave him an odd feeling when he slid into position there. It was the first time in his life he had laid in ambush, determined to kill. Yet it only brought matters full circle. When this all began, he had been the one to ride in under a bushwhacker's gun.

And then began the waiting, whether it was to be for minutes or for hours, with his every faculty riveted to the watch that must now settle things. He would have had it otherwise, but Gilgen had rejected the alternatives out of hand. He pitied the man, even while recognizing the utter deadliness of his enmity. Arliss had never been worth the investment of himself that Gilgen had made in her. She wasn't worth what had to happen now. Hers was the power to arouse passion such as raged in Gilgen, destroying him. She had no capacity to fulfill it for him or for any man.

Pace waited in the mounting heat, his thoughts drifting on to Howie Renner whose enmity was as lethal as Gilgen's, no matter how his baffling sister fitted into the situation. Pace thought about her, too, and why she had imprisoned him in the old mine only to go to the outlaw camp and announce that he was prowling around in the vicinity. Starting a man-hunt when she supposed herself to have the wanted man beyond their finding him.

All at once everything but the immediate situation was swept from his mind. The first warning was a flock of blackbirds that rose from a tree off up the slope, and swept away. Then two men came over the rise, reined in for a quick check forward, then came riding on down the thinly covered plateau. Pace felt his lips pull tight on his teeth. They were the two he expected, and they no longer figured it necessary to watch the ground for sign. They thought

140

they had him aflight on foot and were bound to overtake him before he could reach safety and help.

Pace knew in icy certainty that he could kill them both, almost before either knew what had hit him. That was the kind of consideration either of them would have given him. He steadied himself and let them come well within rifle range. And then he stood up openly to let them know where he was. That was his own and the only way he could do it.

Their horses stopped, the riders staring forward with hard interest. It was something like the confrontation between himself and Baine in Rowel, their surprise robbing them of their aplomb. They only hesitated, and Gilgen was the first to start his horse driving forward. Pace had to watch them both, which they exploited by widening the distance separating them as they drove in. His only advantage was that of elevation.

Again Gilgen moved first, snapping up the rifle he carried across the saddle in front of him. It was a fast, nervous shot, but it was the first to be fired. Pace heard the snap of a bullet and the crack of the rifle before he shot. Howie's shot whipped in and by. Then their rushing horses veered out and away from each other, slanting off from the rocky rise on which Pace stood. It had failed as an attempt to overrun him, but it was still effective. To give his attention to one of them, he had to turn his back to the other. It forced him to drop to the ground.

He expected them to dismount and try to crawl in on him through the low cover. But each of them reined up out of rifle reach and stared toward him and each other. Neither could actually see him, and Pace wondered if either had seen well enough to know whether he had been hit or had dropped down voluntarily. Whatever, he didn't intend to be where they thought he was when they came in again.

He began working himself toward Gilgen, moving carefully through the cover, taking pains not to foul the rifle in the dirt. After the brief spasm of fury, it seemed eerily quiet. He changed location only enough to throw them off, then he waited for what he was sure would be another joint rush. This one would be harder to meet for it would lack the hasty inaccuracy of the first charge. And it would come at him from separate directions.

And then it began again, as if from a signal passed between Gilgen and Renner. They came in shooting, riddling the brush where he had been. Pace let the hoof drum louder until it seemed right on top of him before he rose

141

up to make sure he wasted no part of his small advantage. Gilgen was all but on him. Pace shot and levered to fire again before he saw that Gilgen had grabbed leather.

The horse reared, but Pace didn't know but what Gilgen had forced it up to shield himself. Pace's next shot slammed toward Howie, off to the right, just as Howie fired straight at him. The rifle flew from Pace's hands, bringing a yell of triumph from Howie. Then Gilgen's horse came down and went driving away, Gilgen lurching in the saddle. Howie cut an astonished look toward this. What he saw canceled the advantage he had gained, wiped out his exultation. Very slowly, Tex Gilgen crumpled, slid sidewise and fell to the ground, his horse bolting on.

Pace wasn't aware of having fisted his six-gun until it bucked against the heel of a hand still stinging painfully. A look of frantic urgency on his face, Howie had swerved his horse in the direction Gilgen's had taken. He pumped another hasty shot at Pace, bent on drawing out of pistol range so he could benefit from the longer reach of his rifle.

Dismissing him momentarily, Pace ran to where Gilgen lay limp and unstirring. He held his gun in wary readiness, but there was no mistaking it. The man was dead, shot close to the center of the chest. It was over. Without him, the outlaws wouldn't have stake enough in the fight to hang together. Yet it wasn't over completely, for there was Howie. Pace didn't want to have to kill him, not out of any feeling of mercy but because the man had a sister of a thousand times his value.

Howie had stopped his horse at a cautious distance and was oddly subdued as he stared toward Pace and the still figure on the ground. It seemed to have hit him, at last, that Gilgen must be dead, that without the man to follow, Howie Renner was nobody at all, with nothing to gain whatsoever. He lifted his rifle defensively when Pace started walking toward him. But Pace's lack of furtiveness seemed to tell him it wasn't necessarily a hostile approach.

Pace stopped, barely within earshot, and called forward. "You guessed it, Howie. He's dead. You don't have a thing to gain from pressing this. It could cost you your lousy life. I'm giving you a chance to save it, this one time. Go back to Silver Butte and tell those curly wolves how it come out. Tell 'em I'm sending for the sheriff, and my men will help him clean out everybody left up there twenty-four hours from now. I'm giving you Renners the same period to get gone, once and for all. Tell Jinx that this can go for her or not, depending on how she wants to look at it."

Howie sat motionless, staring toward him. He seemed stupefied. After a long moment he swung his horse and started it moving up the slope to Silver Butte, bewildered and bereft.

Pace caught the other horse, lashed Gilgen's body to the saddle and, leading the animal, started on for the lower basin. Strangely, his knee had quit hurting him. He bore his weight on it heavily, twisted and flexed it, but that symbol of his hatred was gone.

Rather, something close to sorrow lay on his heart. It wasn't for Gilgen, who had refused a rational settlement of their differences. Nor for Arliss, whom he would buy out now to restore the integrity of the Bedrock. It wasn't for Howie and his rudely ended dream, nor for Stella and her bottle. It was for another loner, whose spirit had touched his across the gap of class and sex, a girl he had failed so badly. . . .

It was an hour after dark, and Pace was alone in the big house, when he heard the rap on the front door. Instead of calling out, he went to the door, for he had seen her ride past the light of the bunkhouse windows.

He pushed open the screen and said quietly, "Come in."

She stepped through, and he closed the door and looked at her, too moved for words.

She blinked her eyes against the light and said, "You damned fool. Why didn't you stay where I put you?"

"Why didn't you tell me why you were doing it?"

"I wouldn't give you the satisfaction." Jinx studied her boots. "Then Stella had to go and blab it."

"All she said was that you wouldn't throw the one man around who could tame you, to the wolves."

Jinx looked up, her cheeks coloring. "What girl in her right mind would? Not that I've been in my right mind for some time, though. I sure wasn't when I got the idea that locking up Pace Larabee would hold him still very long." She look at him accusingly. "If you weren't so all-fired lonehanded, you'd have been all right."

"It would have helped to know that."

"You know it now. They were set to hit your headquarters. I stalled that by saying you were prowling around Silver Butte, figuring I had you under lock and key, nice and safe. I had a notion where you left your horse. I got it and was going to show you a way to get home without getting caught. It was your only chance and the only way you could warn your outfit of what was coming. But when I got back with the horse, you'd flown the coop." Jinx

143

frowned in annoyance. "That's the thanks I got for my trouble."

"You wouldn't want me different. Anymore than I'd want you different."

"I guess not."

"But thanks, anyway, Jinx."

"What good did I do?"

"Thanks for finding out, like I did, that no matter what we thought about it, we never hated each other."

She lifted blinking eyes. They were moist. "Looks like we didn't."

"Where are you going now?"

"Where do you want me to go?"

"Nowhere but right here."

"Then that settles it, I reckon."